HOW TO MEET A GIRL (AT THE END OF THE WORLD)

Christopher Compton

Copyright © 2021 Christopher Compton

All rights reserved

The characters and events portrayed in this book are fictitious. Any similarity to real persons, living or dead, is coincidental and not intended by the author.

No part of this book may be reproduced, or stored in a retrieval system, or transmitted in any form or by any means, electronic, mechanical, photocopying, recording, or otherwise, without express written permission of the publisher.

ISBN-13: 9781234567890
ISBN-10: 1477123456

Cover design by: Mandy Roeting
Library of Congress Control Number: 2018675309
Printed in the United States of America

This book is dedicated to my wife, Marlee, who always believed in my dreams, and my mother, who always believed in this book.

SAM'S FINAL MIX

1. Bad Moon Rising - Creedence Clearwater Revival
2. Apocalypse Please - Muse
3. If the World Was Ending - JP Saxe, featuring Julia Michaels
4. California Dreamin' - The Mamas & The Papas
5. Chasing Cars - Snow Patrol
6. Supercut - Lorde
7. The Final Countdown - Europe
8. No Cars Go - Arcade Fire
9. Time to Say Good-bye - Andrea Bocelli & Sarah Brightman
10. Till Forever Falls Apart - Ashe & Finneas
11. How Far We've Come - Matchbox Twenty
12. Apocalypse - Cigarettes After Sex
13. Afterglow - Ed Sheeran
14. Outro - M83
15. It's The End Of The World As We Know It (And I Feel Fine) - R. E. M.

"The images you see now are completely real. This is not a test or a hoax of any kind. As you can see, it's spreading at an alarming rate. Experts and analysts tell us that in approximately twenty-four hours, it will span the entire globe. There is nowhere to run, nowhere to hide. Those responsible are already gone, so there is no one left to blame. All we can do, as brothers and sisters of mankind, is pray, keep our loved ones close, and wait. This news station will remain on the air for as long as possible. To everyone watching, wherever you may be… good luck."

The woman on T.V. keeps talking, but to the sea of confused faces staring blankly at the flickering screen, her words lose their meaning. The school gymnasium is packed tight with teachers, students, the janitors, and principal, but no one makes a sound. A room that big, with that many people in it…it shouldn't be that quiet.

I can hear my phone vibrating. After five or six buzzes, I finally look down. It's her.

➤ *Nathaniel, is this really happening?*

******

THE NIGHT BEFORE...

My phone vibrates exactly when I expect it to. It's become something of a sixth sense in the five months since we started talking. We often joke that we can feel the texts coming, as if we're right next to each other. It's not really a joke for me though. It's more like a wish.

➤Alice: *How goes the party, Mr. Host with the Most?* ☺

➤Me: *I think everyone's having a good time. Sending spring break out in STYLE!*

I watch as people happily dance around my mom's immaculate, blindingly white kitchen. Travis nearly spills his drink while flexing to impress a girl and I wince. This pristine room is my mom's pride and joy, besides me of course. If she came home to find a single stain on the floor, my death would swiftly follow. Thankfully for my life expectancy, if not my state of mind, her globe-trotting job keeps her from coming home very often. She's probably on a plane right now as I use her pet project as a dance floor. Sometimes I think it's kind of nice being alone, having the place to myself. Well, almost to myself.

"Could you get off your phone for once and mingle like a real human bean?" Olivia hollers. "Being. Did I say *bean*? A real human bean!"

She knocks on my forehead like it's a door. Olivia sure feels like an annoying older sister, despite us both being sibling-less. Being three inches taller than me, along with most of the people in our grade, doesn't help the whole 'older-sister-so-I-know-better-than-you' complex.

"Whatever you say, *Olive*," I mutter.

"Don't you dare," she snaps. "Olives are *gross*. Nat, you may be my best friend, but you're turning into one of those phone zombies. Phonbies."

"I thought *I* was your best friend?"

Ezra lumbers over to Olivia and plants a quick kiss on her lips.

"Fancy meeting you here, Tall Girl," he says.

Ezra's the only guy in our school taller than Olivia. To this day, I'm almost one-hundred percent positive that's exactly why they started dating all those years ago, but it's grown into something deeper than that. A lot deeper. Giants in love, I call them. One day, far in the future, they will undoubtedly get married and have giant babies together. It's going to be weird, and horizontally challenging for us short folks.

This rum and coke is making me think weird things. I like it.

"You're my *boy*friend, Poor Boy," Olivia purrs. Those whopping two coolers in her system are really starting to work their magic. "*Best* friends and *boy* friends are totally different categories."

Poor Boy and Tall Girl. Those weird little pet names only ever came out on the rarest, or drunkest, of occasions. Never did hear the origin story for them. Would probably make me puke in my mouth a little. I wonder what pet name Alice would grant me. Maybe we would be one of those cool couples smashed our names together to create a power name. Nathlice. Alilaniel.

Rum and coke. Weird things.

"Boyfriend is a totally *better* category," Ezra replies.

"Speaking of which, I'll be right back."

A thought flashes across his face and Ezra darts off toward the back door of my house. I turn my attention back to my phone and Olivia's curiosity of her boyfriend's sudden departure turns to frustration at my lack of social skills.

"Put that damn phone away!" she orders.

"I'm just telling her we'll talk later," I explain. "God, you're annoying. Go get a different friend to bother."

➤Me: *My friends are forcing me to socialise. Talk to you later!*
➤Alice: *Socializing? During a party? Gross. Have fun* ☺

Travis stumbles over and sloppily wraps his arm around Olivia's shoulders. Shockingly, he's struck out with the girl he was trying to impress earlier.

"He talkin' to her again?" Travis asks, taking another sip of his beer.

"What else is new," Olivia mutters, lifting Travis's arm off her shoulder.

"So lemme get this straight." He points at me and nearly loses his balance. "You and this girl-friend met through Instagram?"

"Yeah," I reply.

"'Cause she liked a picture of you in some cringey, goth weirdo costume?"

"Edward Scissorhands, uh-huh."

"And you been textin' ever since, but never actually met her."

"You got it."

Travis furrows his brow and stupidly looks to Olivia for an explanation to my explanation.

"Oh, Travis," she says with a sigh. "Don't worry your little head. I don't understand this modern love crap any better than you. Could've been worse. Could've been Tinder."

"Bro, if you two are *so* in love, why didn't you invite her to the party?" Travis asks.

"We talked about it," I reply, suppressing the instinct to blush. "Don't want to rush things. Plus, seemed overwhelming, meeting me for the first time… and you, and then everyone else… but mostly you, all at once. Didn't want to scare her off right from the get go."

"We *are* rather disturbing," Olivia chimes.

"Excuses, excuses." Travis pushes me, as if he's daring me to do something. "Can't put it off forever, bro. Eventually, you're gonna have to meet this girl and see if the magic's real."

For some reason, that makes me think of my mom. Like most moms, she is a woman of many, many mottos. When I'm looking for a favourite shirt I've lost, I get hit with 'If everything has a place, then everything should be in its place.' When I'm freaking out over a test I think I've failed, it's the classic 'What's done is done.' But the one that never stuck, no matter how many times she said it, the one that also happens to be her life mantra, now rang through my head like a grocery store announcement: 'Anything worth doing is worth doing today.'

Personally, I prefer the slow, casual build-up. I like to play the long game, but maybe that's just another way of saying, 'I'm not ready yet.'

"I'm working up to it," I mutter nervously. "Just haven't found the perfect moment yet."

"Perfect moment," Travis scoffs, adding a very mature fart noise to punctuate his point. "If you don't hurry up, I'll slide into her DMs and get things done."

"Please don't," I mutter.

Travis shrugs and continues on his way, setting his sights on a new victim to flirt with. Olivia starts looking for Ezra, and I'm left alone. The urge to send another text is overwhelming, but I try to be personable and immerse myself in the crowd.

I hear Dan, the smartest kid I know, and Jeremy, our resident conspiracy theorist, debating something too complicated for my mildly intoxicated mind to grasp. Classic meeting of the inebriated minds.

"I've been over this with you a thousand times," Dan says with a sigh. "The possibilities of discovery vastly outweigh any chance of something going wrong tomorrow. There's nothing to worry about."

"We're meddling with things beyond our understanding," Jeremy counters. "I've been listening to this podcast--"

"Oh my God, you and your podcasts. Here we go."

"Fine. Don't believe me. The end is nigh. Just wait. You'll see. You'll all see."

"Okay, crazy. Why do I bother talking with you?" Dan sees me passing by and lunges away from Jeremy like I'm the life-preserver to his conversation's sinking ship. "Hey, Nate. Didn't expect to see you here."

"It's my party," I reply.

"Indeed. Have you seen Sam around? I brought the comics he let me borrow. Some of them were just dreadful. This one featured haunted vaginas, Nate. *Haunted vaginas.* Can you believe that?"

"I actually haven't seen Sam," I reply after scanning the room. "He might not've come."

"I'll just give them back in class." Dan yawns and rubs his eyes. "I'm gonna sleep through tomorrow, classes and all. Who has a party on a Sunday night?"

"Think of it as practice for next year. That kind of stamina will be expected of us as college kids."

I'm about to explain the tradition of having a party on the last day of March Break when the music changes to a slow song and a loud crack booms from outside. I run to the kitchen window and see fireworks exploding across the night sky. The bright streaks are trailing from my backyard. I don't have to look far to find who set them off.

Ezra bursts through the back door, looking for his giantess. People push past him to go outside and enjoy the show up close. The room is nearly empty, and that's when he locks eyes with Olivia, who is wearing a smile almost as bright as the fireworks.

"It's our song!" she shouts out.

"What a coincidence," Ezra replies after winking at the DJ in charge.

Olivia slowly waltzes over to her giant with a mischievous grin on her face.

"How'd you get fireworks in the middle of March?" she asks.

"Stole them from Disneyland." Ezra looks deep into Olivia's eyes and for a moment, loses his nerve. Even after all the time they had spent together, all the secrets they had shared, she still has the power to make him nervous. "Just kidding, leftovers from Canada Day. I know you hate grand romantic gestures, and you know that I hate them too, so I thought 'what better way to embarrass us both than with fireworks at a party with all our friends.'"

"You truly are the master of embarrassment, Poor Boy."

Her face is close to his, so close he could kiss her, and suddenly, Ezra is calm again. There's something in their eyes that can only be described as the future. They see it all in each other. The way they look at each other—is that the way I'll look at *her* when we finally meet?

"So, my lady." Ezra reaches out his hand and bows. "Do me the honours?"

Olivia bows in kind and takes his hand. They waltz outside and begin dancing under the fireworks. I watch as they twirl in time with the music, and how being in love makes them laugh like little kids. The bursts of light overhead shine upon their faces and with every flash, I see something I hope to call my own one day.

"You're definitely gonna get a noise complaint." In my distracted moment of soapy philosophizing, Sam, out of nowhere, had snuck up on me. "Cops should be here any minute."

"Hey, you made it! Nice to see—" Another firework lights up the night sky, and I see the bruises on his face. "What happened to your eye?"

Sam lets his perpetual slouch take over and hangs his head, allowing his long, shaggy hair to fall over his face.

"I talked back at the dinner table," he mumbles.

"He can't do that—"

"What's going on here?"

He changes the subject and flips his hair back. His eyes are totally dry. He's accustomed to the way things are. I should be too by now, but I'm not.

"Just a little something Ezra put together for Olive," I explain.

"Barf. Hope he saved enough money for the fine you're gonna get."

He watches them dance, and a wistful look creeps through his pained eyes. He sees the same things I do, but it makes him sad; regretful.

"I look at them and just think… I'll never know what that's like," he whispers.

"You can't know that," I tell him. "Life's a long time for things *not* to happen."

"I need something *soon*."

******

Hours later, the party finally starts to wind down. Guests pass out wherever they can find a free spot, or they walk home with a designated buddy. Small-town living allowed such luxuries. I crawl up the stairs to my room, careful not to disturb whoever was having a terrible time in the bathroom across the hall. Miraculously, my bed has not been claimed and I don't have to kick anyone out. I sprawl across that comfy cloud, which has never felt so soft in my entire life.

With a mind of its own, my hand reaches into my pocket and I start texting her.

➤Me: *I'ma little durnk.*

It's very late, and a school night, so I fully expect not to receive a response. It only takes fifteen seconds.

➤Alice: *I couldn't tell ;) Mind if I take advantage of the situation?*

My room is pitch-dark, but the light coming off my phone's screen brightens the night. I can see my face in the reflection, grinning like an idiot. I prop myself up and try to shake the fatigue and intoxication from my mind so that I am at least somewhat intelligible.

➤Me: *Go ahea.*

Close enough.

➤Alice: *What's one weird thing that you like about me?*

Alcohol fuels my fingers faster than I can consciously think about an answer that won't embarrass me.

➤Me: *You always say my full name. Nathaniel. Not just Nate. I dunno. That's something special. Like you're talking to me in a way that no one else does.*

Her response isn't so swift this time. I go over my response again and again while I anxiously wait. With each reading, the text becomes more awful. 'That's something special?' Could I be more cringey? That's worth a ghosting.

After two whole minutes of silence, I am completely mortified. 'You scared her off,' I think. 'She knows you're a weirdo now. No turning back. Just delete her from your contacts and chalk the last five months up to a dream.'

My phone vibrates, and the sudden jolt causes me to fling it to the ground. I scramble to the floor and accidentally flip off my bed. Air pops from my lungs as my back hits the ground hard. Barely able to breathe, I still manage to frantically open her text. What I read makes my heart stop.

➤Alice: *Nathaniel, if I were with you right now, I'd kiss you.*

My fingers twitch, hovering over the electronic keyboard. Did she really just say that? Am I so drunk that I'm seeing things? I lock and unlock my phone, but those magical words stay permanent. I want to say something witty or romantic or anything at all, but my brain locks up. Thankfully, she lets me off the hook.

➤Alice: *Good-night, Nathaniel.* <3

➤Me: *Good-night, Alice.*

Those words on that tiny screen are all I have of her. It's not a dance under fireworks, but it's enough for me. I read them over and over until my eyes give out and I pass out on the floor, hoping to dream of what that first kiss might feel like.

Tip #1: Get a good night's rest. Your last day on Earth will be a long one

24 Hours Remaining

I wake up to the shrill scream of my alarm clock. I try to pry my eyes open, but the devastatingly bright light pouring through my bedroom window keeps them closed. Blindly, I grab my bedsheets to pull myself up, and my sore ribs scream in protest. Why did I sleep on the floor? A dull, throbbing pain brews in my skull, reminding me of the night before.

And with that realization, a slight panic spikes my heart-rate. I unlock my phone and sigh in relief. That electronic promise of a kiss was no dream. There's a new text, too.

➤Alice: *Rise and shine, party animal! A new day awaits* ☺

Alice is always up before me to get her sisters ready for school, so for months, my every morning has started with her. Not even a hangover can spoil a gift like that. Pills and a quick stomach pump might also help.

➤Me: *Can the day wait a little longer? Not ready for it.*

My back aches as I gracelessly stumble down the stairs toward the kitchen in hunt of food. Ezra and Olivia are already at the table, staving off the lingering effects of last night with a shared bowl of cereal. They are attentively watching the T.V. mounted on the wall, tuned into some news channel. I figure it must be something truly extraordinary to take their attention away from morning cartoons, so I grab a bowl of my own and take a seat.

"The updated Mass Particle Accelerator is expected to perform its first major test today," the reporter says in typically dramatic fashion. "It is housed in a Swedish facility deep underground—"

"Sweden," I grunt between bites of cereal. "I think that's where my mom's heading for some big conference—"

Olivia promptly shushes me. With her eyes glued to the screen, the spoonful of cereal intended for her mouth instead collides with her chin.

"Why are we watching this?" I ask.

"Dan was talking about it last night," Ezra replies. "Seemed interesting."

"...top physicists will be attempting to create dark matter for the very first time," the reporter continues. "If successful, this could mark one of the greatest scientific accomplishments in history, and change the very understanding of how our universe was created."

"No pressure," Ezra mutters.

We listen for a little longer while we finish breakfast. We are told that the results of the test will be broadcasted live, but we can't stick around to see them. The dreaded first Monday back from March Break awaits.

I sluggishly brush my teeth and step over the poor soul who has passed out at the foot of the toilet. The day will have to start without her. I quickly stuff my backpack full of books and head to the front door. Being the only one with a car and driver's license grants me the exclusive privilege of chauffeuring my friends everywhere. As I wait for Olivia and Ezra, I take stock of the mess made from last night. Not as bad as I feared, an easy clean-up when I get home after school.

I check my phone and see two texts: one from my mother, and one from Alice.

➢Mom: *On the plane now! Give you a call when I touch down. Love you.*

I try to think of something to say back, but Alice's message distracts me, and I move on without responding to my mom. She's probably in the air by now anyway.

➢Alice: *You're not going to be late for your first day back to school, are you?*

➢Me: *Wouldn't dream of it! We don't have traffic out here in the boonies like you big city folk. Just you watch. I'll arrive with time to spare ;)*

******

Traffic is terrible. Unusually terrible for our small town, in fact. I have never seen so many cars on these tiny streets in my life.

"I didn't think Keswick was capable of gridlock," Ezra mutters from the back seat. "We're definitely gonna to be late for McMahon's class. I heard he made Chloe Fountez cry for missing attendance."

"Maybe there's an accident up ahead," Olivia says.

She leans over from the front passenger seat and flips through radio stations before settling on her favourite pop station. The D.J. – Carlos—is a little obnoxious, but he plays all the best songs from our childhood, so I tolerate him.

"Hey all you listeners out there!" Carlos shouts, punctuated by a silly farting noise played from a soundboard. "We're going all the way back to 2011 for this one, so get those skinny jeans and shutter shades ready! Here comes another hit you love!"

Ezra asks Olivia to pump up the volume while I poke my head out the driver's side window to get a better look at what's causing the traffic jam, but all I can see is a line of cars stuck bumper to bumper. Where the hell is everyone going?

I open my car door and take a step outside, joining a growing crowd of impatient drivers who have also vacated their vehicles in hopes of finding the cause for their delay. As I'm about to take a step away from my car, I hear the sound of an engine roaring. I turn around just in time to see a white van flying up the side of the road at full speed. The driver slams on his horn, but doesn't slow down.

I jump back into my car and slam the door shut seconds before the van howls past. The sound of screams and screeching tires fill the air as the madman narrowly avoids running people down. As the dust settles and the furious honking fades in the distance, those lucky souls who dove out of harm's way return to their feet in a daze.

"You okay?" Olivia shrieks. She tries to check me for injuries, but I push her away in embarrassment. "Is he out of his god damn mind? He could have killed someone! What on earth possesses someone to drive like that?"

"Some people just *really* need their morning Timmies," Ezra jokes half-heartedly.

I grip the wheel and gently press down on the pedal as the cars ahead of me start moving again. My nerves start to settle, but the expression on the driver's face surfaces in my mind and stays there for the rest of the drive. Something about that look, that haunted stare, tells me that he wasn't late for anything. He was running from something.

******

I decide not to tell Alice about my near-death experience. No point in making someone hundreds of kilometres away worry. Besides, we're already late for class, so I can't afford another distracted second. Being run over by a car would be a mercy compared to the scolding awaiting us in Mr. McMahon's class.

"Twenty minutes late," Olivia huffs. She pops open the passenger door before I even put the car in park and jumps out. She's halfway across our school's parking lot before realizing she's left her bag in the backseat. Luckily for her, Ezra takes his time. He calmly hands her the bag, but she's too flustered to thank him. "We're so dead."

"*Dying by your side is such a heavenly way to die*," Ezra sings.

Olivia hustles up to the school entrance with Ezra in tow. The couple dart inside and try to act inconspicuous as they head to class. I'm in no hurry to get yelled at, so I take my time and send Alice one last text before the daily grind begins.

➢Me: *Remember how I said I wasn't going to be late? Might have been wishful thinking on my part. Homeroom teacher's gonna flip out.*

Alice's school has a pretty strict 'no-phone' policy, so whenever we chance conversations during class-time, she's risking her phone getting confiscated for the day. Not quite a modern day Romeo and Juliet, but an obstacle nonetheless. To my delighted surprise, she risks a response.

➢Alice: *Some things never change. Like war. And the joy of popping bubble wrap.*

➤Me: *Bubble wrap will make a good coffin. RIP to me.*

➤Alice: *Don't joke about that. I don't know what I'd do without you.*

I smile and put my phone away. The large steel doors at the front of the school stare me down like a guillotine. I take a deep breath and step inside. Time to face the music. I can practically hear the organ playing as I cross the front lobby.

*Tip #2: Try not to freak out
(this one is hard).*

23 Hours Remaining

Someone else is at Mr. McMahon's desk. The supply teacher looks towards the door as I enter the room and I brace for impact, but she doesn't seem to care about my tardiness. What a relief. I scan the class to find quite a few empty chairs, the least surprising of the bunch being the vacancy at Sam's desk. Not a week went by without him missing at least half his classes. I hope he made it home okay last night. And that his dad left him alone.

Olivia and Ezra are already at their desks, counting their blessings that they did not experience the wrath of McMahon this day.

"Remind me to buy a lottery ticket after school," Ezra says with a smile. He gives me a high-five as I pass by to my seat behind him, next to Dan. "Might be the luckiest day of my life."

"Not like Mr. McMahon to be absent," Dan mutters as I sit down. His fingers tap fast against his desk. "Something's up."

"You're right," I say. "Didn't know robots *could* get sick."

No laughter from Dan. He's distracted, peering out the window at someone running up and down the sidewalk next to the school. The man is yelling something, but up on the second floor with the windows closed, we can't hear him. A woman out for a stroll with her dog tries to ignore him, but I can see that she's frightened.

"Yo teach, mind going easy on us?" Travis asks. He can

barely keep his head off his desk. "Had a rough night."

"You kids treat every Monday like it's the end of the world," the supply says from behind McMahon's desk. She stands up and turns the SmartBoard on. "Seeing as Mr. McMahon didn't leave any notes, I'll take pity on you just this once. We'll watch a Bill Nye video today."

Cheers erupt around the class. The ruckus causes Travis to clench his eyes shut and massage his temples, but he is grateful for such mercy. Out go the fluorescent lights and in a moment the dark is illuminated by the pale glow of a SmartBoard screen. Classmates obnoxiously chant along to the classic Bill Nye intro tune despite the supply's feeble request for silence. I've seen this whole scene play out a thousand times, but it always gets a smile out of me.

"How is it we're in high-school and still watching this stuff?" I hear Ezra ask Olivia. "Can the school not afford new tapes or what?"

"Maybe Bill Nye has some dirt on the schoolboard and forces them to play his tapes until the end of time," Olivia replies. "He's like a master extortionist with mafia ties. Only thing that makes sense."

"Only thing."

Today's very special episode is all about the cosmos. There are jokes and allusions to 2001: A Space Odyssey and Star Wars, but what sticks with me is how long it would take to explore just our solar system. Planets we can see with the naked eye, our very own neighbors, are impossibly far away. Light, the fastest travelling thing we know, still took its sweet time to get around. Four years to get to the nearest solar system, impossible in our lifetime. How small we are, how alone.

It is far too early in the day to get so philosophical over a science show for kids. There might still be some alcohol in my system.

"You ever think about all the things you've never done?" Dan whispers in the dark.

"What?" I ask quietly.

"I don't know…" I can see his face in the half-light of the SmartBoard. His eyes are searching through the room, lingering on classmates, like he's lost. "I've never left the country before. There's so much out there, but I've only seen it in pictures. Isn't that strange? That you can live on a planet so long, but only ever see a part of it."

"What're you talking about? It's just Bill Nye."

The supply gestures for us to stop talking and Dan shuts down.

"Nothing." Dan returns his attention to the man screaming outside. "Just feels like a weird day."

Before I can press him further, the classroom speaker buzzes. The Science Guy is in the middle of making loud, goofy noises, so we can't hear the announcement. While the supply fiddles to find the volume, I can just make out a voice. It's our principal speaking.

"All classes make their way to the gymnasium," he says. The supply mutes the video, so we can hear the announcement clearly. There's a tremor in our principal's tone. "This concerns us all. Teachers, ensure students remain safe, quiet, and calm in the hallways. Please, hurry."

The announcement ends as unceremoniously as it began. Even at the age of seventeen or eighteen, my classmates look to the supply for direction. She seems as confused as the rest of us, but as per Principal Davaron's orders, asks for everyone to line up quietly at the door. Ezra makes a grim face.

"Davaron sounded pissed," he whispers.

"He sounded scared," Olivia mutters back.

"Maybe it's a school shooter, or a bomb threat?"

"We wouldn't be going to the gym. This is something else."

We tuck in our chairs and stand in a line at the door. Dan is the last one out, and he flicks off the lights. There's a haunted look about him, the same look as the driver, as if deep down, he knows what's to come. It makes me uneasy. Out of habit, I reach for the one thing I know will calm me down.

Using cell phones on school premises is highly discouraged, but I've gotten pretty good at bending the rules. Muscle memory guides my fingertips across my phone's touchscreen, allowing me to shoot Alice a text without the phone ever leaving my pocket.

➤Me: *Principal just called a family meeting. Sounds like we might all get grounded.*

I wait for the familiar vibration, but it never comes. My sixth sense tells me she isn't going to respond.

Other classes are lined up in the hall like in a fire drill and teachers are having a hell of a time keeping everyone under control.

"What the hell's going on?" shouts a student, only to be immediately reprimanded.

"Can our whole school even fit into the gym at the same time?" Travis asks.

The huddled mass of students and teachers attempt to navigate the stairs down to the gym without causing a massive traffic jam, but we move at a snail's pace, and the anxiety starts to mount. I can feel it in the air, like the sick anticipation before presenting a project I haven't properly prepared for. Sarcastic jokes die off, replaced by nervous murmurs. I overhear some theories from the crowd around me.

"Didn't Travis break into the school over March Break? Maybe they're doing interviews."

"Probably another boring anti-drug presentation."

"Didn't anyone watch the news this morning? I *told* you guys this would happen!"

"Could be a terrorist attack."

It all sounds wrong or crazy to me. But what else could it be?

The gym doors open and people flood in like herded sheep. Normally, teachers would demand students stay in their assigned rows, but they seem distracted from their duties. Some kids run to their friends, but all those who had arrived first are sitting on the floor, staring, wide-eyed at the front of the gym. The lights are dim and the overhead projector is on. Images from a news broadcast flicker on the gymnasium wall. Olivia and Ezra are ahead of me, and they too are mesmerised. I take a spot next to them, look up, and in that moment, I lose myself to something I don't understand.

We look down upon the world from a bird's eye view. From high above, I see an impenetrable abyss. I can see people on the ground, in cars, on foot, fleeing from the darkness. Scrolling headlines at the bottom of the screen tell me that this is live footage, from somewhere in Sweden, but it looks like a movie to me.

I'm not sure what all the fuss is about, until the black hole expands, and erases an entire city block in the blink of an eye. It looked too real to be a movie. All those people... My hands start to tremble.

Cars, trees, houses, skyscrapers, entire streets are swallowed up as the ever-widening pit spreads across the land at an unnervingly steady pace. Where there should be colour and sound, there is emptiness. Nothing escapes this growing void. A woman's voice from the TV describes the impossible.

"The images you see now are completely real. This is not a test or a hoax of any kind. As you can see, it's spreading at an alarming rate. Experts and analysts tell us that in approximately twenty-four hours, it will span the entire globe. There is nowhere to run, nowhere to hide. Those responsible are already gone, so there is no one left to blame. All we can do, as brothers and sisters of mankind, is pray, keep our loved ones close, and wait. This news station will remain on the air for as long as possible. To everyone watching, wherever you may be... good luck."

The woman on T.V. keeps talking, but to me, staring blankly at the flickering screen, her words lose their meaning. The school gymnasium is packed tight with teachers, students, janitors, and the principal, but no one makes a sound. A room that big, with that many people in it...it shouldn't be that quiet.

I can feel my phone vibrating. After five or six buzzes, I finally look down.

➢Alice: *Nathaniel, is this really happening?*

*Tip #3 : Good-byes suck.
It's okay to cry (a lot)*

22 Hours Remaining (10 Am)

I don't know how to respond. Was the end of the world just announced on live television? Fear grips the crowd around me as the reality of our collective destiny starts to settle in. A boy a few grades lower than me looks up at me, as if I might give him an answer to what he's just seen. I look over to my supply teacher for the same answers, but she has no one to look to. The colour in her face drains out, as if she's just heard the worst spoilers for her favourite TV show.

Our principal stands in front of the projector with a microphone in his hand. The black hole engulfs his face, but I see the tears in his eyes. The newscast is muted so that we can hear his speech.

"I'm so sorry that I have to be the one to tell you this," Mr. Davaron says. He covers his mouth with a trembling hand for a moment. "So many of you are still so young...it's not fair. It's just not fair... For those wondering if this is all true, I'm afraid it is. The Prime Minister has made a statement, confirming that our country, along with the rest of the world, will be... *gone* by this time tomorrow. It is for this reason that I implore everyone to go home—to spend this last day with your loved ones. I wish I had the time to say good-bye to each and every one of you. It was a privilege to be your principal."

Still, no one moves. We stood in place, waiting for instructions, hoping that someone would tell us what to do. Mr. Davaron puts the microphone down and makes his way through the crowd, trying to console students who have started to cry. My mind is still in a spiral. The words on the broadcast, Mr. Davaron's speech, they all keep banging against my mind, but it's not making sense. The world *couldn't* be over. That's not... It can't...

All responsibilities and dreams permanently suspended. The consequences of Travis' hangovers, Daniel's dreams of writing his own comics, Olivia and Ezra and their giant babies; stories stopped before they began.

Then it really dawns on me. My last drive to school was this morning. My last party ever was the night before. The last book I finished reading was over a month ago. When was the last time I went to church? My last fight with Mom...that truth sinks into me like a stone slowly slipping deeper and deeper into the depths of an ocean. We had been doing everything for the last time without knowing. Everything we did, it was for the last time.

Slowly, the crowd starts to disperse as students and teachers regain their senses. I can't take my eyes off the black hole, even as people push past me. The newswoman confirms that the Mass Particle Accelerator is the cause of this calamity. She says the entire country of Sweden will be gone within the hour. The void keeps getting wider and wider, until its edges creep past the boundaries of the screen. It's coming for all of us.

I wander from the gymnasium in a daze. I can hear people screaming. Crying. Students rifle through their lockers, grabbing everything that can fit into their backpacks before darting out of the school. Some teachers stay to ensure the safety of their students. Others flee without looking back. I almost follow them.

My phone's vibrating, but it's not a text. Someone's calling. I look at my phone and although it's not a number I recognize, I instantly know who it is. I accept the call and slowly put the phone to my ear. Her voice is warm and calm. Too calm.

"Nate, is that you honey? Do you know what's going on?"

"Mom!" I shout. I run into the nearest bathroom to get away from the racket in the hallway. Someone is crying in a nearby stall, but it's quiet enough. "Yes, I just saw ... *it* on the news. Are you okay? Where are you?"

"It's nice to hear your voice again," she says. She sounds so serene, like she used to sound right before she would put me to bed. "I wish I could have heard it more."

It sounds like she's talking to herself, voicing some regret that she'd bottled up. Right then and there, I get the gut feeling that this is going to be the worst conversation of my life.

"Why are you talking like that?"

"I'm still on the plane." My ears start pounding and my mouth goes dry. I can hear shouting on her side of the call, people less at peace with what awaits them. "We don't have enough fuel to turn around. There's nowhere to go."

Deep down, my worst nightmares come to pass, and it makes me sick, but I pretend to not know what she means.

"What do you—"

"I can see it." A flicker of fear enters her voice. "Right on the horizon."

"See what?"

Her side of the call goes silent. The shouting and fighting is over. I can hear my mother's trembling breath and in that moment, I see what she sees: a dark horizon. The end of everything. And she's flying right into it.

"We don't have much time," she whispers. She can't hold back the tears any longer, and neither can I. "I just want you to know that you've always made me proud. Your father, too. *So* proud. I hope I made you proud, too."

She doesn't sound afraid anymore. She's happy, at ease.

"Mom?"

"All those promotions and business trips taking me further and further away. It just seems so silly now. The only thing that ever made me happy was you. I wish I could have let that be enough. What I wouldn't give to hold you one last time, even for a moment. Good-bye, Nathaniel. My wonderful boy. I'll see you and your dad soon. I love you."

There is a great hum that slowly turns to a deafening whir, and then nothing. The line cuts out before I can say that I love her too.

"Mom! I love you too. Mom?" I call out, but I know she's gone.

My words never reached her. The phone slips from my grasp and clatters to the ground as memories of my mom rise up like a rush of blood to the head. I'm shaking, crying, pounding my fist on the bathroom floor, but it's not enough. For the first time in my life, I feel truly alone.

I contemplate spending what little time I have left on that bathroom floor, mourning the loss of the person who loved me most in the world, but I fear even then, it wouldn't have been enough.

The latch on the nearby bathroom stall clicks and I remember I'm not alone. Travis exits the stall looking lost, like he had woken up in there. I try to wipe away my tears and act composed, but I see that his eyes are red and swollen too.

"Shit, I thought I was the only one in here," he says, sounding embarrassed. He stands over me with a heavy frown on his face. "Listen, I tried not to eavesdrop. That sucks, bro. Your mom…I can't even imagine. I'm so sorry."

Travis offers me his hand and it takes every bit of strength I have not to break down all over again. I pull myself together and with his help, get back to my feet.

"Thanks," I mutter. I catch a glimpse of myself in the mirror. I look worn out, older somehow. "It's funny. She was never around, but for some reason, I never missed her. Always figured we'd have time to make up for it later."

"Am I going to hell?" he asks, changing the subject so abruptly it nearly gives me whiplash. I turn from the mirror to find that he is being completely serious. "I know…" He sighs. "I know I've been shitty. They say we have a day, right? Well, what if I prayed, like if I spent all day asking—*begging* for forgiveness… would that work? If I really meant it?"

The whole idea is so superficial it almost makes me laugh. Classic Travis. I know he is seeking solace, some comfort that everything is going to work out, but I answer the only way I can.

"I don't know."

Travis nods sadly, as if he knew what I was going to say.

"Guess we'll find out soon enough," he mutters. A smile born of despair spreads across his lips. "Maybe I'll go back home, get my family together, and we'll all spend our last day at church. See if I can get a few brownie points right before the end. Give out bread or something… What about you? Any big plans for your last day on earth?"

What an impossible question. The last hours of my life left up to me, and I don't have the first clue of how to spend them. I always wanted to go to Peru and climb the steps of Machu Pichu, ever since I saw it in a magazine as a little boy. The architecture looked ancient and otherworldly at the same time. But Machu Pichu would be gone before I got there.

I thought I'd study to be a history teacher after highschool, or maybe a lawyer—to help archive forgotten texts or navigate the choppy waters of corporate law, but those texts would be forgotten now no matter what. Who cares about law now that the world is in chaos? Everything I've ever aspired to be or dreamed to see is lost.

But I can't just do nothing. Then, I see my phone on the floor with a new message flashing on the screen. The tiny words on the screen are simple, but they hold all the answers.

- Alice: *Nathaniel? Are you still there?*

Mr. Davaron's words of spending time with loved ones rings in my head, followed by my mother's mantra, calling out to me. 'Anything worth doing is worth doing *today*.' With both my parents gone, I had no family left, no responsibilities to the future to worry about, but despite this black hole taking everything from me, I didn't need to spend my last day on earth alone. Someone is out there, someone who cares about me.

In that moment, my mind shifts into a different gear, and it all becomes clear.

"Alice," I say. "I'm going after her."

"What? The Instagram chick? You're not serious."

"Says the guy who wants to spend his last day singing choir songs," I reply. He chuckles a little, but I can tell he still doesn't get it. "What you said last night, you were right. I can't put it off forever. That perfect moment is now."

Travis is stupefied, as if I've suddenly started speaking another language. Weirdly, his skepticism, while totally understandable, doesn't inspire the slightest inkling of doubt in me.

"As romantic as that sounds," he says, "you've never even met the girl. You've got one day left, less than that. Is seeing her *that* important?"

"Honestly, it's the *only* important thing I can think to do today."

"But there's no point."

"Was there ever?"

Travis is at a loss for words, but he can tell by my determination that there was no swaying me.

"Okay," he says. He pulls me in for a great big bear hug, and I don't resist. Mostly because Travis is much stronger than me and I wouldn't have been able to pull away if I wanted to. "Good-luck, Nate."

It's been years since he called me by my name. I kind of wished he had said 'bro'.

"You too," I whisper.

Travis releases his grip, but I don't let go quite as quickly. This is the last time I will ever see him, a childhood friend since playdates were a thing. I can remember his face as a seven year-old so well. He still has that look of mischief he had back then. As he grew older, he became a bully to some, sure, but he was a bully who always had my back. That had to count for something when all the points were tallied.

I stoop down to grab my phone from the floor, and as the bathroom door closes behind me, I hear Travis mutter to himself:

"The world *would* end on a Monday."

******

The hallway is no longer gripped by chaos, but the after-effects are even more unsettling. An eerie lull has fallen over the school, like the calm right after a big storm, or right before an even bigger one. Teachers and students wander in and out of empty rooms with hollow looks on their faces. A lone janitor attempts to clean the papers and notebooks strewn across the ground, as if it was just any other day. Reminds me of the band playing as the Titanic went down.

I check my phone. My battery is draining, along with what time I have left before the end arrives. My heart is pounding and every cowardly instinct I have tells me to back out—to just spend my last day going over the regret of never meeting Alice again and again in my head. It would be easier.

I send the text I should have sent five months ago.

➤ Me: *Still here. Forgot to mention something.*

She responds immediately.

➤ Alice: *What??*

➤ Me: *I'm coming to see you today. I think we're long overdue for that first encounter.*

The message barely finishes sending before my phone starts vibrating. Alice is calling. My finger twitches involuntarily and before I know it, I'm answering the call.

"Nathaniel, what the hell are you talking about?"

The gentle quiver of her silksong voice is so warm, so close, like she's already with me. I can see her deep brown eyes and the slight curves at the corners of his lips. I'm on a cloud high above the ravenous dark, with her. We're holding hands. Nothing can touch us. We're free.

"Hello to you too," I say. Couldn't have sounded dorkier if I tried. "Nice to hear your voice."

"Do you know what's going on out there?" She sounds confused, anxious. "They're saying it's the end of the world."

"Sure looks that way." I wonder what my mom would think, knowing her son is planning on driving out into a world on fire. My breath catches for a moment, but I force myself to only think about being with Alice, no matter how crazy it might be. "You'll be the last thing I see when the world goes dark. Can't think of a better way to say good-bye to this life. That's why I'm coming to see you. There's nobody I'd rather spend the apocalypse with than you, Alice. I love you."

That's the first time I've ever said it out loud to her, and it's as easy as breathing. I thought I'd be scared, like 'staring-into-a-black-hole-that's-eating-my-entire-planet' scared, but I'm not. I'm just so glad that it's her.

"I love you too," she says back. She laughs, and it's the most beautiful sound I've ever heard. "You're fucking crazy, but I love you, Nathaniel."

We both take a moment to laugh, like giddy idiots who haven't a care in the world.

"Is that a 'yes, I'd love to see you?'" I ask.

The pause that comes next is much longer. I can hear shuffling and the murmur of quiet voices. Alice returns to the phone and lets out a deep sigh.

"Of course it's a yes," she says. "But we should meet in the middle. Not fair of you to come all this way. I just need to say good-bye to my parents and sisters. What about your mom?"

A lump forms in my throat at the mere mention of her. Our last conversation tries to replay in my head, tries to make me relive that terrible pain, but I cast it aside as a tear streaks down my face.

"I've already lost her," I say. My voice sounds wooden.

"Oh, Nathaniel, that's awful--"

"So I don't have any reason to stay here. But you should stay there."

"Nathaniel, I'm not--"

"We need to be with the ones we love, so you should be with your family until I get there. And that's why I want to see you, more than anything. A silly little extinction event isn't going to stop me."

My own courage catches me off-guard. I've never heard myself sound so certain before. The black hole will steal everything from everyone, but it's given me the kind of confidence you only muster once in a lifetime. Maybe it's all false nerves, some biological response to facing down certain death, but I'm not missing my chance.

"You're amazing, but if I stay here, you won't make it," she tells me sadly. "There's too much distance to Toronto, traffic will be insane—"

"I'll make it, Alice. I promise."

"Okay. I'll be waiting. Please be careful."

That's it. After five months of school, part-time jobs, busy schedules and other stupid excuses getting in the way, my course is set. I hang up the phone with a smile almost too wide for my face to hold. My head is spinning as I run up the stairs to raid my locker. I'm going to see her before the lights go out. I'm going to see Alice.

******

"Damn it."

The lock requires precision, and even though I've input the same combination a thousand times throughout my high school career, my fingers are too jittery to operate the dial. To be fair, I have a lot on my mind: the death of my mother, saying good-bye to all my friends, and going off to see the girl of my dreams before a black hole envelops everything. Not ideal circumstances for calm, rational behavior.

After my third failure, I lose patience and try to rip the lock clean off. Shockingly, it works. Small miracles.

"Thank you, cheap school lock," I whisper.

I grab my backpack off its hook and toss it to the ground, loading it up with everything I will need for my travels. The snacks I had packed instead of a real lunch, my phone charger... Wait, where is it? Hefty textbooks crash to the floor as I turn my locker upside down in search of a phone charger that I slowly realize isn't there. I must have forgotten it at home in the mad scramble not to be late for school.

"Damn it!"

Before I can expel more frustrated expletives, I hear someone's sneakers squeaking up a storm in the hall. It's Jeremy, our resident conspiracy theorist, and he looks absolutely ecstatic.

"I knew it!" he yells out in vindication. "I said this would happen and nobody believed me! You all thought I was crazy, but look at me now! The end is nigh! See you in the great beyond, foolish mortals!"

Jeremy bangs on lockers like drums as he does laps around the hall, stopping here and there to break out in a little dance he must have prepared for the end of days. I watch him dart down the stairs to spread his glad tidings to more non-believers. At least someone is having a good time.

Someone taps me on the shoulder and I nearly jump out of my skin.

"Sam!" I yelp. I lower my voice a few octaves and assure my heart there is nothing worth exploding over. "Jesus, man. Why you always gotta sneak up on people like that?"

"Sorry," he says, looking off in Jeremy's direction. "That dude once got an M & M stuck in his ear and had to melt it out with a hairdryer. Being right about this whole mess doesn't make him any less of a nutcase."

I laugh, which surprises me for two reasons. For one, discovering that laughter doesn't have to be extinct in an apocalypse was a bit of a shock, but even stranger was who had brought that small joy into the world. Sam was never really the bringer of levity, even on his best days. I can see that something is different about him. His shaggy hair is the same, but it's pulled back out of his blackened eyes. The world can see his bruises, and he doesn't seem to care.

He's also brought a handful of popcorn with him, which I am almost certain is stolen from the local movie theatre.

"I thought—"

"That I'd stay at home with my loving father and you'd never see me again?" A mischievous smile twirls upon his lips as he pops another kernel into his mouth. "As if you'd ever be so lucky. Nope, you're stuck with me until this day is done, my friend."

I shake my head.

"I'm not sticking around. I'm going to see Alice."

"Somehow, I think we all saw that coming," he says, unfazed. "And that's why I'm here. I'm going to help you get to her in time."

Something is *definitely* different. Sentimentality was hardly Sam's strong suit. I look him over and start to quantify the subtle changes. Gone is his perpetual slouch, like a weight lifted from his shoulders. There's a buoyancy about him now, like if he left the ground he might never come down.

"What? Why?" I ask. "This is it—the last day you'll ever have. You'll never get a chance to do anything else. Don't you want to do something for yourself?"

"Maybe this is me doing something for myself," he says. He picks at his collar, which for him is a sign of embarrassment. "In a way. Or maybe this is me paying you back for all the times you stuck by me when I was a total downer. You never deserved that."

I don't know what to say, but the first thing that blurts from my mouth is the complete opposite of what I wanted.

"What about your dad?" I ask. "You're seriously just gonna leave him?"

Sam's face hardens to stone.

"Screw him," he growls.

"Sam, he's family."

"I know. Screw. Him. The only signs of affection he gave me are ones like this." Sam points to his swollen eye. There's a tear running free from that purple prison. He wipes it away, hoping I won't notice. "We didn't care for each other before the world's end, no point in starting today. Only thing I care about now is getting you to this Alice person. Just let me tag along. Let me be a part of something good, just once."

Sam looks like an abused puppy begging to come in from the rain. How can I say no to that?

"Well," I whisper, "what are we waiting for?"

"You!" Sam exclaims, and immediately he is light-hearted once more. He finishes off his popcorn and wipes the crumbs on his pants. "Dumbass. Get your shit together and let's go. Get this show on the road already."

It feels good to have someone tagging along for this crazy little quest of mine. I would have willingly spent my final day in isolation if it meant spending a moment with Alice, but Sam's company, while unexpected, is more than welcome.

I notice that a margarine container is conspicuously tucked under Sam's arm. Strange in and of itself, sure, but the guarded way in which he's clutching it begs to be questioned.

"Hey, uh, Sam, what's with the butter?"

He shifts to the side, trying to hide it.

"Just hurry up," he says.

I finish packing my bag and slam my locker shut. The lock's broken, but anyone who wants to loot my extensive collection of overdue library books can have at it. Sam and I sprint down the hallway and dash into the staircase. Every second that passes is one less I get to spend with Alice. It pushes me to run faster than I should. I take the final flight of stairs too quickly and lose my footing.

If Dan hadn't been there to catch me, I might have done some serious damage to my ankle.

"Holy crap," I gasp, clutching my heart in an attempt to calm it down. "Thanks. Nearly became a tragic PSA against running down stairs. Saved my life."

"For what that's worth," he mutters.

He's wearing the same despondent look he had back in science class, only this time, there's no frustration or shame. There's nothing but an empty husk.

"What's the matter?" I ask.

"What's the matter," he scoffs. "That's a funny question to ask at a time like this... Just this morning, I was freaking out over a math test and prepping my college application. Now...this. None of it mattered."

"Of course it did," I say unconvincingly. "You weren't wrong to—"

"Easy for you to say," he snaps. "Let me guess. You're going to see Alice?" I nod. "Thought so. See, I don't have anything like that. I played the game all wrong."

"We couldn't have known."

"Looking back, it was kind of obvious."

With heavy feet, Dan walks past me up the stairs. I want to stop him, to prove him wrong, but I don't know how. He opens his backpack and takes out the comics he borrowed from Sam. Dan laughs a little before giving them back.

"Thanks," Dan whispers. "I really liked a few of these. Was hoping to write one of my own one day."

He continues climbing up the steps in a daze, to where, I don't know, but I have a sinking suspicion that if I don't try to reach him, I will never see him again.

"It's not too late," I call after him. "You can come with us."

He stops at the top of the staircase. I can't see his face, but I hear his voice.

"Alice believes you can make it." It wasn't a question, more like a chastising rebuke. "And you believe too. Good luck, I guess."

With that parting wish, Dan quietly left the staircase, and let the door to the top floor close behind him.

******

Sam and I spring through the back door like it's the last day of school. Not quite how I had imagined graduating, but it's still a rush. I try not to dwell on all the memories locked up in that old building, how many notes I had passed around in secret, how many exams I had passed by the skin of my teeth. Still, it's hard not to look back one last time.

"Don't get nostalgic on me now, Nate," Sam says, pushing me toward the parking lot. "We spend too much time focusing on what we're about to lose, we'll never get to see what's ahead."

He's right, of course. I don't want to spend these last hours reminiscing on what was. There's still plenty to look forward to.

Sam and I reach the car and I fumble through my pockets for the keys. The parking lot is pretty empty, save for the cars of the less favourable teachers who hadn't reached their vehicles before spurned students. Their tires are slashed, windows smashed, and their seats full of wet toilet paper. One particularly mischievous student is in the middle of spray-painting a message across the windshield of Mr. Davaron's SUV.

Mr. Davaron sux dicks!

"Clever," I say.

"Just be thankful no one mistook your rust-bucket for a teacher's car," Sam says.

"I'd be happy to take your Lamborghini on this adventure," I shoot back. "Where is it again? Oh wait, you don't have a car."

"Low blow."

We climb in the car and close our doors in unison. When

I turn around to back out of my parking spot, I pause. The backseat is empty. The car suddenly feels too quiet.

"Holy shit," I gasp. "I totally forgot about Ezra and Olivia. We have to go find them!"

Sam looks past me, and a smile shapes over his lips.

"You don't have to look very far."

I spin around and right outside my window are the two giants wearing hopeful smiles. My heart is put at ease. In all the commotion, I hadn't thought of how Olivia and Ezra would fit into this wild ride, but truth be told, this trip will be a whole lot better if they come along.

"I wasn't gonna leave without you guys," I say truthfully. "Seriously, my mind's just been—"

"Sure you weren't," Ezra says with a wink.

The apocalypse hasn't seemed to faze them one bit, like they've already come to terms with it. By the way Olivia is fidgeting with her hair, I can tell she has something she wants to say. It's not like her to hold back.

"Nate," she whispers. She looks to Ezra and he nods. "There's something we want to ask you."

Ezra rubs Olivia's back to comfort her. She takes a deep breath and her words run together in a rush.

"We ran into Travis and he told us your big plan. I think it's great that you're going to see Alice and I don't want to get in the way of that, but we don't have a car and we'll never make it in time. I know it's far, and not quite on the way to Toronto, but it's where we met and it seems fitting. Poor Boy and I had our 'first date' there. Always thought we'd get married there, too. It's where we want to be when…" She takes another big breath. "It's Wasaga Beach. Can you take us?"

Wasaga Beach. It *is* far, and it *isn't* on the way to Toronto.

It would add an hour or two to the trip, even if traffic is good. That would mean an hour or two less time with Alice. But I look to the two giants to find them fighting back tears. Ezra wraps his arm around Olivia's shoulder and she keeps her chin up. They look down on me through the driver's side window, eagerly awaiting my response.

These are my best friends, people I've told numerous times that I would do anything for. And I know they would do the same for me.

"What about your families?" I ask. There's a lump in my throat. "What will they think?"

"Oh, they'll be pissed when we tell them," Olivia croaks with a bitter chuckle, "but I'm sure, deep down, they'll understand."

"It's like Davaron said," Ezra adds. He looks to Olivia and presses his lips to her cheek. "If this really is the end, we should spend it with that one person that makes it all seem a little less terrifying."

Olivia turns to Ezra and puts her lips on his. That kiss, the way they hold each other, and how the world disappears around them—that's what this is all about. Before the end, I want to find my own piece of that comfort.

"We'll make it work," I tell them. "I'll get you there."

Sam makes a barfing noise as he unlocks the car doors.

"Welcome aboard," he groans.

The two giants thank me profusely and hop into the backseat. Once I hear their belt buckles click in place, I slam my foot on the gas pedal and burn some rubber. I had always wanted to do that on school property. I'll have to mail my thanks to those dead scientists in Sweden first chance I get.

As I pull away from my school parking lot for the last time, I look into my rearview mirror. Someone is on the roof of our school, looking out to the horizon. No one sees him but me. Is it Dan? I can't tell. Just as I turn the corner, he jumps off, head-first, and I close my eyes. That will not be me. That is not how I say good-bye to this life.

"What's with the butter?" Olivia asks.

Tip #4: Take only what you need. Leave the rest behind

20 Hours Remaining

"Someone's gotta be working on a way to stop it."

My friends clutch their phones close, combing through limitless layers of information for some semblance of sense in all the chaos. Phone service is getting really spotty, likely overloaded with billions of people trying to reach each other, so most of us have switched to different messaging apps instead of conventional texting or calling. I keep my eyes glued to the road. News of global annihilation spreads quickly, and fear has turned our tiny town into a madhouse. Traffic moves erratically and civilians on the sidewalk are even less predictable, running out into the street without warning. As much as I want to, I can't exceed the speed limit, and my foot constantly wavers over the brakes.

"How do you stop something like that?" Sam scoffs. "Can't exactly throw a net around it. Just gotta close your eyes and hope it doesn't hurt."

"Are we sure this black hole is even real?" Olivia asks.

"For the millionth time, it's not a black hole," Ezra chimes in. "That's not how they work. Scientists say---"

"Are these the same scientists that just Thanos-snapped our whole planet out of existence?" Sam asks. "Or are these the not dead scientists? Hard to keep track. Looks like a black hole, acts like a black hole, it's a black hole to me. If they want to come up with a better name, they have less than a day to do it."

"Anyway!" Olivia chirps. "Like I was saying, are we sure this is even real? Maybe it's some kind of global prank or social experiment."

"It's on every channel, every radio station, every inch of social media," Sam replies. From my peripheral vision, I see pictures and videos flash across the screen of his phone as he endlessly scrolls through his news feed. "I don't think *'it's just a prank, bro'* is gonna get us out of this one. There's no escaping it. It's real all right."

"Trust me," I mutter. I swerve to avoid hitting a group of kids haphazardly crossing the street. "It's real. My mom was still in the air this morning. I was on the phone with her when it… took her away."

Sorrow casts the car in a silent spell.

"Oh, Nate," Olivia whispers. Her words shudder from her lips. "I'm so, so sorry."

Collectively, my friends pay a silent moment of respect to my mother.

"I didn't know her that well," Ezra says, "but I remember she made the *best* grilled cheese sandwiches. Like, I don't know what kind of cheese she used, but it even *smelled* amazing."

"She would make them when I was home sick from school," I say. "'Better than soup,' she would say. Not sure if that was true, but I always felt better after…I'm just glad I got to hear from her one last time. And I'm glad you're all here now."

Olivia reaches from the back seat and squeezes my shoulder. I look into the rearview mirror and see her wipe a tear from her cheek. I place my hand on hers and squeeze back.

"By the way," I say, "how did the whole... telling your parents you're never gonna see them again thing go?"

Olivia retracts her hand and her face turned dour. She looked to Ezra who flashed a reassuring smile, but I can tell that he too is hurting.

"Yeah," she mutters. "That wasn't a fun conversation either. They were... less understanding than I had hoped."

"Sounds like we could use some of that dope grill cheese right now," Sam mutters to himself. He sees something on his phone and becomes entranced. "There's this trend on TikTok of the best black hole plunges. It's called the See You on the Other Side challenge. Best one I've seen so far is some dude in Norway back-flipping off a building as it gets swallowed up. What a bad-ass Norwegian."

I see the footage from the corner of my eye. The black hole, impossibly high and overwhelmingly wide, slowly encroaches up a small city street. A shirtless man with enormous energy, likely fueled by drugs, or alcohol, or a cocktail of both, gives his camera an enthusiastic wave before flipping off a skyscraper into the abyss below. He's gone before he hits the ground, just like that. No screams, no blood. Poof.

"I need to think of something to top *that* when I go out," Sam says.

He laughs and tosses his phone into the backseat for Olivia and Ezra to see the clip. His flippant attitude casts furrowed brows on both the giants. Olivia ignores the phone and gives Sam a sideways look.

"Something seems different about you, Sam," she notes.

"Ah, well," Sam grunts. "Today is a different kind of day. Everyone knew the path the old Sam was going down. No one can predict me now."

Olivia knows I'm looking at her in the rearview mirror and does little to hide her apprehension. Sam spins in his seat to face me with the twinkle of an idea in his bruised eye.

"Let's make a pit-stop at your place," he says.

"We don't have time," I reply.

"It's on the way out of town. We need to grab snacks for the trip and besides, you said you forgot your phone charger. You'll need that baby at full battery for this journey." His suggestion is sound, but it's his next point that really sells the argument. "Besides, do you really want to meet Alice *and* die in your school uniform?"

I look down at myself and imagine meeting the girl of my dreams in a baggy, navy blue sweater and dull, grey pants that always managed to give me a wedgie.

"My house it is."

******

For as long as I've lived, my neighborhood always had a quiet, borderline boring atmosphere surrounding it, like a time capsule from the 1980s. People walked their dogs, mowed their lawns, watered their gardens, and waved when someone passed by. Raucous house parties, or noise of any kind past eight o'clock, was a rarity. But if today was your first visit to my neighborhood, you would never know that bland paradise.

Today, smoke fills the air.

Families are in their driveways, packing up their cars with as much as they can carry. People I don't recognize run into my neighbors' houses and come out hauling electronics ripped right from the walls. As I pull into my own driveway, I am both surprised and relieved to see that my front door is still somehow intact. The nice robbers must have been saving my house for last.

My friends and I exit the vehicle and cross my front lawn like maneuvering through a lion's den, careful not to draw any unwanted attention. With time ticking away and threat of a break-in at any moment, we will have to be quick once inside. I unlock the front door and step inside my home.

"All right, everyone," Sam says. "Grab what you need. Nothing bigger than a bread box, and let's be outta here in five minutes flat. Break!"

He slaps Ezra's ass like they're in a locker room and dashes toward the kitchen. Olivia and Ezra look to me as if to ask, 'what's gotten into him?' but I just shrug it off. My cell phone charger is in my room, making it my first destination. I take the stairs two at a time on my way up and only manage to trip once. New record.

When I reach the top floor, I hear a noise coming from the bathroom. Someone gagging?

I slowly open the door to find a remnant from last night's party. Marissa, I think her name is. The toilet bowl cradles her head and when I flick on the lights, she winces in pain.

"Sorry," I whisper, turning the lights back off.

"Ugh," Marissa groans, keeping her eyes closed and her head down. "What did I miss?"

"The world's ending," I explain gently. That came out blunter than I wanted it to. "Today."

Marissa pulls her head from the toilet and forces her eyes open to squint at me. She sees how scared and serious I am and groans again.

"Sure feels that way," she grumbles. "Mind if I stay here a while?"

"Take all the time you need."

Marissa returns her head into the sanctum of my toilet. I give her peace by quietly closing the door on my way out. My bedroom is right across the hall, but another room calls out to me. *Her* room, the one at the end of the hallway.

The room pulls me into its warm embrace and I feel safe. No other room in the whole house feels more like home. Dust falls from the ceiling over her empty bed, the same bed I would run for in the middle of the night after having a bad dream. I can see what looks like a pale waterfall in the sunshine pouring through the half-opened window. When I move through the room, the dust chases after me. She has dozens of awards and trophies spanning decades of her illustrious career, I know she does, but I can't find them anywhere. All I see along the walls, on her dresser, by the windowsill, are pictures of us.

There's a framed picture of me and her sitting on the

night table right next to the bed. My ninth birthday. I'm wearing a comical little party hat, the ones that have string neck straps, and looking right at the camera. My dad was never in the pictures because he was always taking them. My mother, however, is right by my side, looking down at me. I'm smiling for the camera, that earnest, but strained kind of smile. Hers is so natural, so genuine and beautiful.

I remove the picture from its frame, fold it in half, and put it in my shoe to keep.

My nostalgic haze leads me down the stairs and into the blindingly white kitchen my mother adored. I think back on the painstaking hours she poured into perfectly painting those walls, all the effort she spent scrubbing every minor stain clean. Its brilliant luminescence blurs the edges of the walls and cabinets to the point where it no longer feels like just a room. Today, it feels brighter than ever before, a bastion of light. Would this one spot remain a haven from the coming darkness, or would it be lost like all the rest?

I hope it outlasts everything. After all, it holds a very special memory: The first time I ever 'met' Alice.

******

"Hon, we're going to be late," my mother says.

She hustles around the kitchen in her business attire, doing four-hundred-twenty-seven things at once, while I sit at the table, trying to balance eating breakfast, watching T.V., and scrolling through my phone all at once.

"When are we ever late?" I reply between mouthfuls of cereal.

A notification pops up at the top of my screen. Someone new has liked the Halloween picture I posted from a few weeks ago, the one where I'm dressed like Edward Scissorhands. I look through the likes; Olivia, Ezra, Travis, and someone I don't know. Someone named Alice Moreau. Pretty name. I click on her profile to see how well the face complements the name.

"Wow."

Cereal slips from my lips back into the bowl as my mouth momentarily hangs open. Even on my tiny cell phone screen, she's a looker. Deep brown eyes, a wide, beautiful smile, and an indescribable aura around her that makes me feel like I might have met her before in a dream. Deciding that further investigation is warranted, I creep through her listed likes and interests to gauge how well suited we would be for one another. Loads of horror movies, The Office, Salvador Dali, no country music in sight. More hits than misses. Many more. A promising prospect.

"Nate, hurry up!" my mother urges. "Unless you want to take the bus?"

Half of me hears my mother's warning and takes action by putting my unfinished bowl of cereal in the dishwasher. Milk splashes everywhere, but I don't really notice, because the other half of me is still entranced by this wondrous mystery that has swooped into my life. Maybe she's just a big Tim Burton fan, I rationalize. Maybe her liking my picture is just a gesture of respect for the artistry of my costume. Or maybe...

Before I can talk myself out of it, I've opened DMs with Alice Moreau. The blank box beckons to be filled with that crucial first message, but my mind's just as blank as the box. It needs to be something cute, but not creepy; endearing without being overbearing. Such a fine line to walk. Don't screw this up, don't screw this up, don't screw this up!

Alice Moreau beats me to the punch.

➤ *Alice: Nice costume*

My heart stutters to a halt. Now I know I must be awake, because not even my dreams go this well. Despite my general lack of experience in the fine art of talking to girls, my response comes on like an instinct.

➤ *Me: Thank you random internet stranger! I made it myself. Like you, I'm a big fan of all things Burton.*

Random internet stranger. I read my message again to make sure. Yes, I actually wrote that. Was I trying to be funny? If funny was a target, I missed it by a mile. Shockingly, an ellipsis—the telltale sign of a returning message—pops up. Apparently I haven't crashed and burned just yet.

➤ *Alice: How do you know I like Tim Burton? Creeping through my profile already, eh?*

Oops. Tipped your hand way too early, Nate. How am I going to salvage this one?

➤ *Me: My parents always warned me against talking to internet predators, but they never said I couldn't BE an internet predator. Ha! Loophole.*

A little cringey and contrived, but for the most part, I assess the banter as successful.

➤ *Alice: You are a very clever predator. I would be honored to be preyed upon by you :)*

"She's cute."

My mom is craning her neck to get a glimpse over my shoulder. I try to quickly and discreetly shove my phone into my pocket, but by the sly grin on her face, I can tell that the damage has been done. She knows. Mom always knows.

"Mom, please," I mutter, trying to act nonchalant by packing my lunch into my bag. "Snooping is strictly prohibited. Pretty sure there are privacy laws in place specifically against mothers for this very reason."

"Are you going to ask her out?" she asks, tongue firmly planted in cheek. "How do you know her?"

"Calm down with the questions, detective," I say, but the idea of Alice and I together forms in my head and suddenly I'm the one that needs to calm down.

"Okay." My mother leans against the kitchen counter and wears a knowing smile, like she can already see exactly how this story is going to end. How do moms always know? "Let's start simple. What's her name?"

No escaping this awkward confrontation. She would just find out sooner or later anyway. After suppressing the urge to flee from the kitchen, I reluctantly withdraw my phone and the moment my eyes make contact with the screen, I'm at ease again. Deep brown eyes. Beautiful smile. Somehow, I know: This is the girl of my dreams.

"Alice. Her name is Alice."

******

"Holy crap!" Sam's shout drags me from my memories.

I race to the kitchen to the sounds of splashing. The cause of the calamity is none other than Sam, rummaging through the fridge a little too vigorously. Cranberry juice runs across the laminate tile flooring like a winding river, splitting off and staining red in every direction. If my mother were still alive, she would have killed us both.

"Oops," Sam says with a grimace. He waits for the hammer to come down, but I'm too numb to care. He resumes pillaging ripe treasures within the fridge with glee, packing bananas and pears into a bag. "I bet nobody ever saw this coming. I mean, I'm sure most people knew the world was going to end *eventually*, but it's not some far away time off in the distance anymore. It's a real day now." He paused and smiled at me. "It's today."

"You make it sound like a good thing," I say, throwing a wad of paper towels on the mess of juice, as if my mother might walk through the door at any moment to reprimand my sloppiness.

"I can think of worse things. I mean, think of all the disappointment we just side-stepped, the diseases we cured, the wars we avoided; all the pain that was just washed away into... nothing."

He says this with the giddiness of a child counting his presents on Christmas morning.

"You're way too excited about this," I mutter.

"Why shouldn't I be?" he asks with a smile. "No one will ever be scared again, or sad, or alone. This will ease everything. Everyone gets a blank slate."

"Except we don't get a chance to start over. It's total annihilation. It's the end."

"Or the beginning of something new."

Our little philosophical debate is interrupted by the back door bursting off its hinges. The door crashes to the kitchen floor and three intruders step into my home. Looters. Two guys and a girl from the looks of it, but their masks, the ones people wear at creepy masquerades or *Eyes Wide Shut* parties, makes it hard to tell.

Upon seeing Sam and me, the intruders freeze. Apparently, they had not been expecting company. They have baseball bats and brass knuckles. We have fruit.

"Cool masks," I whisper nervously.

The looters say nothing. My eyes fall to the empty cranberry juice container at my feet. I pick it up and feebly brandish the plastic container at my attackers. They don't seem impressed. They take a step toward us. This isn't going to end well unless I try something.

"You can take whatever you want," I say. "We won't fight you. There's no point. It'll all be gone by tomorrow anyway. Why are you even doing this?"

The looters are quiet for a moment, but with their faces covered by masks, I can't tell if my words mean anything to them.

"I drove by this neighborhood on the way to work every week," the looter closest to us says. His voice is muffled by the mask, but I can still hear his sadness. "Sometimes I would stop to get a better look. All the fancy things I never had. Now, I get a taste."

"Hey, guys, we heard some banging—"

With their hands full of goodies for our adventure, Olivia and Ezra enter the kitchen from downstairs, ignorantly stepping right into the fray. Seeing the looters, their arms go limp, and their haul spills onto the floor.

I brace for violence, expecting the looters to pounce on the two giants for their sudden appearance, but strangely, they stay put. The looter in front raises his hand up, as if he's surrendering. Are they allergic to cranberry juice?

From my peripheral vision, the barrel of a handgun stretches out, pointing straight at the looters. Still clutching his margarine container close, Sam brushes past me, holding the looters in his sights. I want to say he's an action hero swooping in to save the day, but the gun is rattling in his hand. His finger is twitching back and forth over the trigger.

"L-leave," he stammers.

The two looters in the back don't wait for a second invitation. They practically trip over one another as they bolt for the backdoor. The leader of the pack holds his ground, staring directly at Sam. I hear him laugh behind his mask.

"You don't have the guts, kid," he says.

Sam takes another step forward.

"Try me."

The looter takes off his mask to reveal a grizzled beard highlighted by a cutting smirk. He's old enough to be my dad. Seeing the man's face causes Sam to slightly lower his gun, but enough for the man to notice. He shakes his head.

"Word of advice," he says. "Don't pull that thing out unless you plan on using it. You could get hurt. Next time, no hesitation. Fire away."

The man drops the bat in his hand and leisurely strolls out the backdoor without looking over his shoulder. The second he's gone, Sam instantly drops his arm and exhales deeply, like he'd been holding his breath the whole time. I know I was.

With wobbly knees Sam walks over to the looter's bat and tucks his gun into a holster hidden under his shirt. How had I not noticed that before?

"I think this'll do you better than a juice bottle," he says, tossing the bat to me.

My senses have yet to return, so I miss the catch and let the bat rattle to the floor. Olivia and Ezra just stare at him.

"What the hell, Sam?" is all I can think to ask.

"Huh? Oh, the gun." Sam pulls it out again to show off. "Pretty badass, right?"

"Very badass," Ezra declares breathlessly. He strides across the kitchen to get a closer look. "Where the hell did you get a gun?"

"Under my dad's bed," Sam replies. He inspects the weapon with a hint of disdain and fear. "Stupid drunk thought I didn't know he had it, but I did. Grabbed it when I heard the news before I left for school. Figured it would come in handy today of all days."

"Is it such a good idea?" Olivia asks. "I know it just protected us, but do you even know how to use it? What if it's *our* heads you end up blowing off?"

"Just be ready to duck," Sam says.

The joke lands with a thud. The way he shook when he held it, and how his finger quivered next to the trigger plays again in my memory.

"Olivia's right," I say. "It's too dangerous. We don't need it."

"We *just* needed it," Ezra says. "Who knows what those dudes would've done if Sam hadn't scared them off."

"They were here to grab some stuff and get out," Olivia says. "Pulling the gun escalated things if you ask me. Besides, how many times are we going to run into people like that today?"

"Better to be safe than sorry." Sam tucks the gun back into the holster. "We've wasted enough time arguing about this."

"Sam," I snap. He sighs and looks straight at me. The way he spoke to me at my locker gave me the impression that today, he would do anything for me. Let's see how far that power extends. "Promise me the gun stays only as a last resort. I don't want to see it again unless it's absolutely necessary. Got it?"

Sam stares at me for a moment, reluctant and stone-faced. I can't tell what he's thinking, but he can see how serious I am about this. Slowly, he nods.

"Okay," he says. "Whatever. Now, go change already ya goober. What the hell were you doing up there anyway?"

My mother's room had distracted me from the real reason we had come to my house in the first place. No phone charger and same old school uniform.

"You don't want to look like a good little Catholic school boy the first time you meet this girl of your dreams," Sam teases, "unless that's her fetish or something."

"At least he gets to change," Olivia mutters. "I'm gonna die in this dorky uniform."

"Good thing I don't have to," Ezra says. "Mind if I borrow some clothes, Nate? Preferably ones that don't look like a crop-top on me?"

"Absolutely."

"Not fair," Olivia says.

Ezra and I hurry back up to my room and prepare to change into something a little more appropriate for a 'first date.' We don't have hours to fret over the perfect outfit, so my lucky sweater and favourite pair of black jeans will have to do.

"How do I look?" I ask Ezra.

He stops raiding my closet for a moment to analyze my attire. He's always been a better judge of style.

"You'll knock her dead," he says with a smile, which

quickly turns sour. "Nate, I didn't get a chance before. Are you sure this is what you want? All this running around. You could just stay with Olivia and me and Sam."

"What do you mean?"

Ezra pulls a shirt from its hanger, one he had bought me for Christmas three years ago. Along the front, in bold red lettering, read 'If zombies eat brains, we'll all be fine.' I always knew he secretly wanted that shirt for himself. Neither my mom or my school found it particularly appropriate, so the shirt didn't see the light of day very often. Plus, it was *way* too big for me. When it was just me and Ezra hanging out, though, I always made a point of wearing it. Ezra rubs the soft fabric with his thumb and looks at me as if he's sorry.

"I don't want you to feel that you have to meet Alice because you have no one else," he says. "You have us. Mr. Davaron said we should be with family. We could be your family."

He shrugs shyly. He's never been great at the whole 'expressing your emotions' thing. He usually left that heavy lifting to Olivia. In fact, I can't remember the last time it was just me and Ezra, alone, talking about our feelings. I can't help but feel a little guilty.

"I know," I say. "I'm so happy to have you guys, and I don't want you to feel that you're not enough, but Alice and I…we had all these plans, you know? I was going to take her to all our favourite spots. Eat a nice, greasy burger at Big Dave's, head down to the pier at midnight to watch the stars over the lake, show her that hill where we filmed that terrible video for Mrs. Philip's English class." We share a quick laugh at the reference, despite the fact that we both came down with awful colds the day after filming. "It's my fault… I know it is. I waited too long to share all those places, those memories, with Alice. But if I can just get one moment with her, anywhere on this earth, it won't be so bad. So you're off the hook, mister."

I punch Ezra gently on the shoulder and smile.

"Okay," he says. "We're with you. Whatever it takes."

Without further delay, Ezra changes while I stuff my phone charger into my pack. I glance at the clock on the wall before exiting my bedroom, never to return. A half hour has slipped by since our arrival. Didn't even feel it go.

"You two good?" Sam asks as Ezra and I rush down the stairs.

"Let's get out of here," I say. I want to look around the house I grew up, to take it in one last time, but I can't. "No more pit stops. The beach and Alice's house. That's it. We can't afford anything else."

My friends grimly nod in agreement. Judging by how they had all packed their bags to burst with food, blankets, pillows, spare clothes, and anything else we might need, like we're going camping through Europe for a month, we would be fine. It was only one day after all.

There's no point in locking the front door as we leave, but my mother's voice pops into my head, scolding me for being so careless. Guiltily, I go back and correct my mistake, despite knowing the back door was lying on the kitchen floor.

We pile into my car, which thankfully has been left alone in our absence. My neighbor's house, now ablaze, isn't so lucky. A hooded figure holds a long stick with a skewered marshmallow up to the roaring flames.

"Did Dan say if he liked them?" Sam asks, blissfully ignorant to the destruction around us.

I look over to find Sam reading through the comics Daniel had returned.

"I don't think so," I reply, flipping the ignition and putting the car in reverse. "He mentioned something about haunted vaginas?"

"Yeah, that was a weird one."

With a heavy foot, I pull out from my driveway fast enough for the tires to squeal. I shift the stick into drive and hit the pedal. A potent force pulls at me as I speed away. My eyes drift from the road ahead, back toward my home. I swear I can still see that blindingly white kitchen through the window, and a shadow behind the curtain, waving good-bye...

"Nate!" Olivia screams.

I slam on the brakes and my car comes to a screeching halt inches away from a small dog who has wandered out onto the road. I'm on the verge of a heart-attack, but the dog doesn't even seem to notice how close it came to being a pancake. The teddy bear in its mouth is singed almost to a crisp. It dawdles away, but I'm left shaking too hard to move.

"Let's try to keep flattened puppies to a minimum on this trip," Olivia huffs. I feel her hand on my shoulder, reassuring. "We'll get there, Nate. We will. In one piece, please."

"So, elephant in the room," Ezra whispers. "How long *do* we have? I know Davaron said tomorrow, but that's kind of vague."

"News says the world will come to a total end sometime tomorrow morning," Sam answers, scrolling through his phone. "The darkness seems to be spreading outward, not inward. Lots of jargon about rotational shifts and grav-gravi—"

"Gravitation?" Ezra suggests.

"Gravitation, thank you," Sam continues. "Basically, a lot of science shit I don't get, but it looks like the rate of expansion isn't getting faster and, lucky for us, we're about as far away from the epic-center as anyone can get. Estimates put a black-out for Canada around dawn." He puts his phone down for a second and looks out the window. "To think, some people only had hours, minutes even, before it all went dark…we'll still be around for the last sunrise this planet ever gets."

Slowly, I lift my foot off the brake and let the car roll back up to speed. I scan my rearview mirror for the abandoned dog, but I can't see it anymore. All I see is my neighborhood going up in flames. I shift the rearview mirror away from me and focus on the road ahead.

"Let's make it count."

Tip #5: Let all your secrets be known. Because, why not?

19 Hours Remaining

Life on the road during the apocalypse, we discover, is rather difficult. I constantly have to ignore suggestions made by the onboard GPS as all major routes into Toronto are clogged with traffic and there's absolutely no time for daydreaming, as street-side disputes threaten to spill onto the road every few seconds. Every time I ask Olivia to update Alice on our progress, I'm forced to slam on the brakes. This time, it's because a pack of looters are carrying a conga line of stolen goods from an electronics store.

"Why bother stealing?" Ezra asks. "It's not like the black hole is going to have good wi-fi."

"It's like that looter-guy said," Sam replies. "They want something they never would have had. Live like kings and queens for a day. Or maybe it's just for the thrill of it. Could be stupid people doing stupid shit for no reason, though. Who knows? Who cares?"

"Take a right off Glenwoods onto Woodbine," Olivia instructs, using her phone as a map. Having a part-time job on the outskirts of the big city last summer means she has the most navigational experience. "If that's packed, go up Ravenshoe to Warden. We'll just keep going over until we find a street no one knows about."

Olivia's optimism clashes with the evidence before us. Every road we find is congested with an endless stream of cars, each undoubtedly possessed by some desperate notion similar to ours: righting one last wrong or saying sorry to someone who needed to hear it, or finding the perfect place to die. My perfect place is with Alice. In her arms would be a nice bonus.

"With this many people on the planet," Ezra says, "someone's *gotta* be working on a way to stop it. Or there's some cave somewhere that all the rich, important people are hiding in."

He just keeps repeating the same phrases of disbelief, but I know better than to hope for some last minute Deus Ex Machina. I think back to what I had seen on that projector in the gymnasium; infinite, expanding emptiness.

"I don't know," Sam mutters. He's been mostly quiet since leaving my house, preoccupied by headlines on his cell phone. "I kind of hope we can't stop it. I take comfort in the fact that no matter who you are, or what you do… today is the day the world ends. Famous actor? CEO Billionaire? Doesn't matter, you're dead too. Nothing can stop it. We're all going out together. Which reminds me. I have something for just this occasion."

He unzips his bag and after some scuffling, retrieves a CD case with a homemade label. He pops it open, hands me the CD, and flips the case into the back seat for the giants to see. There's marker on the disc that reads "Final Mix".

"You have a playlist for the apocalypse?" Ezra asks.

"You don't?" Sam replies. I pop the CD into the slot.

"Can't say I really planned for scientists to open up a black hole that would eat us all, so no, I don't."

"See, now you just look unprepared."

Ezra reads out the set-list as the first song comes on. I recognize it instantly. *It's The End of the World as We Know It (And I Feel Fine)* by R.E.M. Generic and predictable, but pretty much mandatory.

"*If the World Was Ending* by JP Saxe featuring Julia Michaels, obviously, *How Far We've Come* by Matchbox Twenty, *Bad Moon Rising* by CCR, don't know that one, *Apocalypse Please* by Muse, more indie garbage only Sam likes I imagine, *California Dreamin'* by Mamas & Papas, *Time to Say Good-bye* by An-Andrea Bo-something I can't pronounce—"

"Wait a sec," Olivia interrupts. "The rest make sense to me, but how the hell do *California Dreamin'* and *Time to Say Good-bye* fit in on this list?"

Sam turns to the backseat as if he's about to give some grand lecture.

"For one, Ezra you embarrass yourself by not knowing CCR. Secondly, *California Dreamin'* just straight up *sounds* like the end of the world with that slow tempo and melancholy chorus."

"Everything sounded like that in the sixties," Olivia retorts.

"Exhibit B," Sam continues, "the singer gets on his knees and pretends to pray, but he knows that it's not going to make a difference because it's already too late."

"Or maybe she just doesn't really believe in it."

"As for *Time to Say Good-bye*, also known as *Con te partirò* according to a Wikipedia search—"

"Oh, Wikipedia, how official—"

"The song is talking about going away to distant lands that don't exist anymore, how there's no light on the horizon, and that it's time to say good-bye. Sounds fitting to me, especially considering our current circumstances. Plus, that song makes me cry, every time."

"I'll give you that one, but I'm still not sold on *California Dreamin*.'"

"Good song, though," Ezra chimes in.

We enjoy Sam's mix-tape for a while, debating the inclusion of certain songs over others, and occasionally singing along with our favourites. I ask Olivia to text Alice for me, as she has agreed to facilitate our conversations for the remainder of the journey under oath that she won't creep too deeply into our past conversations.

"Ask Ali what her favourite end of the world tune is," Sam says as the CD switches over to a song aptly titled *Apocalypse* by Cigarettes After Sex.

"Ali sounds so weird when you say it," I say as Olivia sends out the text at Sam's request.

"That's her name though," Sam replies.

"It's Alice, actually."

"I'll leave the long-form to you two love-birds."

"Shockingly, like most people from planet Earth, Alice doesn't have a favourite end of the world song," Olivia replies sarcastically. "She says, 'I don't have one. I've been more into love songs lately.' Aw."

"I don't know what to tell ya, Nate," Sam says with a sigh, "I don't think she's *the one*."

That gets a big laugh from everyone, except Sam, who is too deeply involved in his phone to realize what's so funny.

"What're you looking at?" I ask.

"People are posting some really embarrassing shit on Instagram and Twitter," he replies. "How self-obsessed are we to spend our last fleeting moments broadcasting our dirty little secrets on social media? And people are eating it up! It's like our generation's campfire stories."

"Isn't that exactly what you're doing?" Olivia asks. "Eating it up?"

"No. This is different. This is scientific research."

"Oh really? Researching what?"

"How people react differently to their impending doom. Lots of interesting data."

"Shut up and share the juiciest ones."

"Well, apparently that rumour about Chloe Fountez was *true* after all. She really did get a black eye by running into a tree over the Christmas break."

"Really?" Ezra says. "I thought Travis started that rumour as a mean joke because she turned him down."

"He did," Sam confirms. "Just happened to be right, co-incidentally. Broken clock syndrome. Also, Rebecca was sexting teachers and then blackmailing them for better grades."

"That little slut," Olivia snaps. "I *knew* something was up when she started beating me in law class this year. Mr. Pratchet, you dirty pervert."

For the first time since hitting the road, Sam put away his phone. He turns to us with an expectant gaze.

"Now it's our turn," he says.

"Our turn for what?" I ask.

"To share our best kept secrets," he replies. Olivia groans. Ezra and I share similar reactions. "Come on. Nothing leaves the confines of this car. Not like anyone will be around to tell in a few hours anyway."

The sea of red tail-lights on the road ahead forces my foot to the brakes once again. I look to Olivia for redirection, but I can tell from the exasperation in her eyes that we are running out of options. How many streets did we have left? Sam was right. We had nothing to lose, except time itself.

"Fine," Ezra says nervously. He pauses for a moment as if to reconsider, but after a deep breath, he starts spilling. "I'll start. I, uh, steal cases of Ginger Ale from the local Food Mart at least twice a month. My parents are kind of busy with two jobs each, so one of my chores is to pick up food every week. First time I stole a case by accident. Just left it at the bottom of the cart and didn't ring it through. When I went outside, the alarms didn't go off. So the next time I went grocery shopping, I put another case at the bottom of the cart and walked right out. No one noticed. Nothing happened. Haven't paid for Ginger Ale in over two years."

"Stolen Ginger Ale?" I ask. I can't help but laugh. "That's the best you've got, Danny Ocean?"

"What?" Ezra shoots back, embarrassed. "Sorry, I don't dive eye-first into trees or send dick-pics to teachers in my spare time."

"Well, I think it's sweet," Olivia says, pecking Ezra on the cheek. "Plus, it's good to know I'm not dating some serial dog molester. I guess I'll go next. Hm, something good. Oh! I've been using a fake ID to get into R-rated movies at the Gem Theater for the past two years. Never been caught."

"Boring," Ezra moans. "That's not a secret."

"What?" Olivia is genuinely shocked. "Who knows?"

"Literally everyone," I say. "Pretty sure the people who work at the theater make the fake IDs to get more business. Did you get yours from Dale?"

Olivia pouts.

"Yeah," she mutters. "He used to work there."

"Sorry, my dear," Ezra says. "You're not as sneaky as you think."

"Well, I thought it was kind of cool."

"Someone else go."

"I tried to poison my dad once."

The car goes quiet. There's some nervous laughter from the backseat, but it dies swiftly. Sam is looking out the window, peering out across the open country fields. He holds his margarine container close as he tells us his truth.

"He was never my biggest fan, even less so when he found out I was batting for both teams. That really got to him, I think. When mom was still around, she would keep him in check. She would protect me," he whispers in a detached tone, like he's sharing a story he heard from someone else. "You always see in the movies, the dad's been drinking when he goes off on his family. Not my dad, not back then. He was completely sober, knew what he was doing....anyway, something stupid, like how I wouldn't eat my peas at dinner, would set him off, and I'd hide in my room with my dog Chester until morning. He was always bad, my dad, but something about *her* being there kept the worst of it away. But that's a lot to put on someone, day in and out, no breaks, for the rest of your life. So, she left. I don't blame her. I would've done the same."

We listen to his story, silent. Sam never spoke of his mom.

"Things got worse, after that. My dad started to drink then, a lot. According to him, it was my fault she left, of course. I tried to be the good son, say 'yes sir, no sir, sorry sir,' take every step like I was walking on thin ice, but it didn't seem to matter. He'd find reasons to stay mad at me, to put me down. Every night was like this intense stand-off. Dinner would come, and those… fucking cold, mushy peas would be on my plate. You know, I think he served them because he knew I hated them. Even if I *tried* to eat them, he'd see the look on my face, that I wasn't enjoying it, and without mom there…I would still hide in my room with Chester, after. That pupper always had my back. Sometimes, if I was lucky and my dad wasn't looking, I'd feed Chester my peas under the table. He was like this little vacuum made only to eat peas. And lick my bruises until morning, I guess. Sometimes I'd use him as a pillow. For years it was like that. But I got older, bolder. I took over the dinners, the cleaning, even some of the bills part-timing at the grocery store. I could take care of myself. I didn't need him anymore. That's when I got a bright idea."

Sam stops, and from the reflection of the passenger window, I see a tear slide down his cheek.

"You guys ever watch *Breaking Bad* on Netflix?" he asks. A sick feeling hits me in the gut as I nod. "Turns out there's this poison, ricin, that's pretty easy to make. Tasteless, odorless. Perfect. Not like he'd notice even if it wasn't. So one night, two years back, I wait for him to get home, and I have dinner ready. I put it in the peas because he knew *I* wouldn't eat them. I'd get beat, sure, but after a few days, he'd be gone, and it would look like he just had a really bad flu."

Sam stops looking out the window. His eyes fall to the margarine container in his lap.

"But he wasn't hungry that night," he whispers, so quiet I have to hold my breath to hear. "I tell him he has to eat. He looks at me funny, the same way he'd look at my mom sometimes, like he's happy I'm there to look after him. So he sits down, and I'm holding my breath with every bite he takes. He eats his meat, his mashed potatoes...but not the peas. With a straight face, he apologizes. For what, I'm not sure. 'Never liked peas, to be honest,' he says. 'Just thought you should eat your greens'. He scrapes the peas off under the table, right into Chester's mouth. I watch my dog gobble them down like he always does, but there's nothing I can do. My dad gets up, ruffles my hair, and thanks me for dinner before going to watch T.V. Chester's staring up at me, tail wagging, patiently waiting for my scraps. He has no idea."

Olivia is crying in the backseat. Ezra is in shock. Chills run through my entire body as Sam finishes his story in the same detached tone he started with.

"I lie with my dog in my room for the next two nights as the poison gently runs its course. I try to make him throw it up, but he won't eat anything. Chester gets sicker and sicker. My dad doesn't know what's wrong. I want to tell him so bad, or take him to the vet, but I can't. They'd know it was me, and I'd be screwed. On the last night, I use him like a pillow like I used to. I feel his chest rise and fall, slower and slower. And then it doesn't rise anymore. We buried him out back right before I had to go to school the next morning."

I've known Sam a long time, almost as long as Olivia and Ezra, but it always felt like there was a barricade between us, some part of him that no amount of friendship could unlock. Hints would drop here and there, and I would fill in the blanks the best I could, but my friend remained a guarded mystery to me. I always thought that if I broke through somehow, we'd be closer. Now that the truth is out, all I feel is sadness, like I never really knew him at all.

Sam looks right ahead into the red sea of tail lights and smiles sadly.

"We look at ourselves in rose-tinted mirrors," he says. "Never forget that you're a worse person than you remember. This darkness that's coming? We deserve this."

No one knows what to say. We just stare in silence at the endless stream of red lights in our way. Sam rolls his shoulders back and resumes his chipper disposition.

"So, who's next?"

Tip #6: All plans will fail. Make it up as you go along

18 Hours Remaining

"**G**uys, look."

Endless traffic on every road we try has forced us far off course, with each diversion taking us further from the main highway, deeper into farmland territory. Houses and stores make way for rolling hills of dirt covered in what snow is left from winter. That lingering snow, rapidly melting since March Break, puts a heavy mist in the air. But in that mist, there is no sea of red tail-lights. There's no one out here but us. For the first time since our journey began, the way is clear.

My friends all lean forward with looks of disbelief. It's like the world's already empty.

"Does this road take us all the way to Wasaga?" I ask.

"We've taken a lot of detours, but it'll get us close enough," Olivia replies, consulting her GPS. "If it stays like this, we'll be there by sundown!"

Cheers erupt through the car and I can't help but breathe easy. I was beginning to worry we wouldn't make it at all, but if I can drop Olivia and Ezra off by dusk, that should put me with Alice before midnight. That gives us almost half a day together if we don't sleep. Easiest all-nighter of my life.

We've reached the end of Sam's Final Mix CD and due to popular vote, which mostly comprised of Olivia complaining that she didn't want to hear the same songs again, we switch back to D. J. Carlos, who miraculously has retained his charisma in spite of a world-ending event.

"D. J Carlos here playing the hits all the way into the apocalypse!" the radio host announces. "The world may be ending, but the party's just getting started!"

"I wonder what drugs he's on right now," Ezra says. "Probably all of them."

"Why are there no cars out here?" Sam asks.

"We're in the middle of nowhere," Ezra replies. "Or maybe people are starting to get where they need to be."

"Whatever it is," I say, "I'm just glad we finally caught a break. Olivia, please inform Alice that we are now hauling ass."

I hear Olivia clicking on my phone, sending out my message. I hate that I have to use her like that, and that there's now *another* space between Alice and me, but it's the best I've got. It will all be worth it when I get there.

"I've been meaning to ask," Sam says, eyeing me with suspicion. "How do you know you're not being catfished right now?"

"'Scuse me?" I ask.

"Like what if we get to her and she's actually some 45-year old fat dude named Stan with a hairy back and a Tim Burton fetish." He's only half-joking. "Would be a hell of a way to find out, right at the end of the world."

"Then maybe you can make out with your dream guy right before everything fades to black," I shoot back. "Won't even hurt my feelings."

"He does sound like my type, huh?"

Sam leans back in his seat and lets the fantasy play out in his mind. I notice the clicking from the back seat has stopped. I look in the rear-view mirror to see Olivia staring back at me with the distinct air of mischief. Uh oh.

"Sam brings up a good point," Olivia says.

"That's a first," Ezra quips.

"No, really. Nate's kept Ali from us for far too long. You know what? I want to talk to this girl. I say we call her up and put her on speaker phone."

"Right now?" I ask, flustered.

"Now is pretty much all we've got," she replies.

I try to think of excuses, like how I needed to conserve my phone battery, or how I didn't want to take time away from Alice and her family, but then it hits me: This is the only chance my friends would get to interact with the girl of my dreams. This is my one shot at uniting the people who gave me my best memories with the person who would have made my future so bright. Who am I to get in the way of two worlds colliding?

"All right," I concede. Before my friends get too excited, I lay down the law. "Ground rules: This isn't twenty questions. I don't want the three of you bombarding her for the gritty details of our relationship—"

"Ha!" Sam bursts into a fit of laughter. "You used the word 'relationship.' Do you guys have like, phone sex?"

"See, I already don't want him to be a part of this," I grumble. "You would have been the last person Alice met, if at all."

"Rude," Sam mutters.

"Shut up, Sam," Olivia snaps. "Nate, continue."

"Secondly," I continue, "no sharing embarrassing secrets about me. That's privileged access. Keep the conversation away from my butterfly collection, or crying in Mrs. Plunkett's class after people made fun of my butterfly collection, or my weird fear of hair in my food, or that unfortunate bathroom mishap at gymnastics, or—"

"Yeah, yeah, we got it, Nate," Ezra interjects. "We'll keep her image of you squeaky clean. We're not all animals, like Sam."

"Double rude!" Sam decrees. "I would never—okay, the fear of hair thing is a public service announcement that I feel all significant members of your life should know about. It's fucking weird, and it's my duty to inform Ali of what she's getting into."

"Did anyone bring duct-tape?" I ask. "For his mouth?"

Sam mimes zipping his mouth shut and throwing away the key. Olivia and Ezra wait with barely controllable anticipation for me to make the call.

"This is a mistake," I complain. "Big, terrible mistake."

Mistake or not, I nod to Olivia to make the call. She presses the speakerphone button and the loud sound of ringing fills the car. The moment I hear that irritating noise, my palms start to sweat over the steering wheel. No answer after the first ring. My heart is thumping like a jack hammer. No answer after the second ring. My friends' eager eyes bore into me. The third ring is cut short by the divine sound of her voice.

"Nathaniel, is everything okay?" Alice asks.

"Hey, it's—uh yeah, no we're fine," I reply, completely tongue-tied. Sam mouths the word 'smooth' and gestures for me to get on with the introductions. "I have some people here that'd like to meet you. You're on speakerphone, by the way."

"Is that so?" Alice says in a playful tone. "Thanks for telling me before I said anything incriminating. Who's on the other end?"

Nobody speaks. My friends are looking at me like deer in the headlights, even though this was their idea. I wave my arms for someone to step in and Olivia awkwardly takes initiative.

"Olivia here!"

"She prefers Olive," Ezra chimes in much to his other half's annoyance. "Ezra, by the way. Nice to 'meet you,' finally."

"Nice to meet you, too," Alice replies. "Nathaniel isn't exactly punctual with introductions. Or anything, actually."

"You call him 'Nathaniel?'" Sam slathers my full name in ridicule. "That's... cute."

"Let me take a wild guess," Alice says, keeping her cool a lot better than me. "Sam?"

Sam looks at me with a distrusting eye.

"What've you told her about me?"

"Only good things," Alice replies quickly. Everyone laughs but Sam. "Nathaniel has nothing but the best to say of his friends."

"I'm sure he exaggerates," Ezra jokes.

"Ezra? Olive?"

"Olivia, and yes, we're here."

"Nathaniel mentioned he had a stop to make along the way. Does that mean I won't be meeting you in person?"

"Unfortunately," Ezra says. He shares a melancholy smile with his giantess. "Wasaga's our last stop. It's where we met."

"How romantic," Alice whispers in a wistful tone. "I would've liked to hear that story."

"Maybe we'll tell you when we get there," Olivia says.

"How close are you to the beach?"

"Traffic has been ass, so we had to take the long way," I tell her. "But now we have a pretty clear shot. Shouldn't be much longer."

"I seriously can't wait. My family's been so focused on the end. My sisters are... It's just getting kind of sad over here." She pauses for a moment, and my mind immediately starts filling in the blanks. I think of my last conversation with mom, and how that must feel stretched out over an entire day. Alice takes a deep breath and continues with renewed enthusiasm. "But I have something to look forward to. I got you a present."

"You did what?" I ask. "What mall is open today?"

"I didn't buy it. I kind of made it myself. Not much of an artist or a craftsman, but I think you might like it."

I don't know what to say. Who thinks to do something like that at a time like this? I look to my friends and find them all smiling, even Sam. Seems that Alice just earned herself some brownie points from the friendship committee.

"I... didn't get you anything," I confess.

"Such a romantic, isn't he?" Sam teases. "I'd say he's like this with all the other girls if there were, ya know, other girls, but lucky you, Ali, the first of your kind."

"Wait, first?" Alice asks. "First as in... Nathaniel, you've never...with anyone?"

The car goes quiet. I slowly look over to Sam and contemplate unbuckling his seatbelt and pushing him out of the moving vehicle. He doesn't budge, as if he stays completely still, I might not notice him.

"You two have been talking for five months and this never came up?" Sam mutters. He turns to the backseat as if he's looking for something. "Okay, then. Where did we put that duct tape?"

"It's not that, I, well you see," I stutter, trying to get my footing on some path to a logical sentence. "Sam is on drugs."

"Yep, all the drugs for me," Sam says. "Don't listen to a word I say. Too many drugs."

"Well," Alice says, stretching the word out so long I thought it might snap along with my brain. "You know what they say; you never forget your first."

Sam mouths '*gross*' and I punch him hard enough for the car to swerve a little. He motions for me to keep two hands on the wheel and I mime hitting him again.

"You mean, you don't care?" I ask.

"Why would I care?" she replies. "I mean, I'm gonna have to edit my present a little bit, remove all the references to past girlfriends, call off the hookers, hopefully get my deposit back, but shouldn't be a problem."

Everyone else in the car is laughing, but it takes me an extra beat to realize Alice is joking. I eventually convince my brain to laugh along with them instead of having an embarrassment-induced panic attack. Crisis avoided.

"Hookers on the last day," Sam whispers, smacking himself across the forehead. "Why didn't I think of that?"

I'm about to fish for some clues as to what this mysterious present might actually be when I see something in the distance that makes my heart drop. Piercing through the mist like the eyes of a dragon is the too-familiar red glow of tail lights. The way ahead is blocked. I bang my fist against the steering wheel and reluctantly bring the car to a stop.

"What was that?" Alice asks.

"Nothing," I lie. I look to Olivia for a redirection, but by the grim expression on her face, I can tell that there's a hard conversation ahead. With Alice's hopes so high, I decide it's a conversation best held in private. "Can I call you back? My battery's getting low."

I've never had to lie to Alice before. It feels completely unnatural, like diving deep underwater and taking a long breath. My insides are on fire. Worse, I can tell she knows something is wrong.

"You're sure everything's okay?" she asks.

"Yeah, we'll be at Wasaga soon." My lying voice is about two octaves above normal, so I try to divert her attention and end the call as quick as I can. "Then it's straight to your place. Can't wait to see my present. And you, of course."

"Of course," she says, sounding slightly less wary than before. "Have a safe trip everyone. Sam. Olivia, Ezra. Looking forward to that story. Nathaniel. I love you."

"Love you too," I say quickly.

I nod for Olivia to end the call. As soon as I hear the beep, my rage comes rushing out.

"Shit!" I yell. "God damn traffic every bum-fuck nowhere place we go. I thought we were past this!"

I pound my fists across the steering wheel while letting more expletives fly. My friends stay quiet, patient for the storm to pass. After sufficiently swearing myself out, I take a few calming breaths and collect my thoughts.

"Did you just say the L-word to Ali?" Sam asks.

"Now where do we go?" I ask, knowing the answer will be bad.

"That's it," Olivia whispers. "This was the last road. There's no other way."

"There's *gotta* be," I snap. "Look harder."

I want to snatch her phone away, prove to her that there's some path she's overlooked, but I know there isn't any.

"Nate," she says softly. "I'm sorry. We have to turn around. Or wait here."

I reflect upon how many streets we've already attempted, and how much time we would waste retracing our steps.

"We can't go back," I mutter. "And we can't wait here."

The car goes quiet for a while as we collectively think of a way out of traffic hell. Teleportation is the only thing coming to my mind. If only the technology had been developed a little sooner. Another killer pick from D.J. Carlos pulses through the speakers. I'm not familiar with the tune, but it seems to spark an idea in his mind.

"Where we're going, we won't need roads," Sam says in an airy, almost reverent tone.

"What?"

He rolls down his window and points out across an empty farmer's field. It's too early in the year for crops, so there's nothing but dirt clumped into bumpy little hills. Sam pops his head back in the car, eyes wide, like he has just discovered a stairway to heaven.

"Off-roading!" he exclaims. "We're taking this bitch where no cars go. Think about it. We'll bypass all these people, make a straight shot to the beach, and save a shit-load of time that you can spend canoodling Ali."

We all stare at him blankly. The car stereo goes silent as the song ends, as if it too is processing his suggestion.

"Canoodle?" Ezra whispers.

"Let me get this straight," I say. "You want me to drive out into that bumpy-ass field with tires I'm almost positive can't handle it, in a car you just hours ago described as, and I quote, 'a rust-bucket.' That's your plan?"

He ponders the pieces of this particular puzzle for a moment, and then gives a lively nod.

"Yeah."

I look to the backseat for opposition, just the slightest hint of resistance, or any sort of argument that would sink this plan for the spectacular failure it would no doubt be.

The two giants shrug and nod along in agreement. Sam smiles.

"Brilliant," I mutter.

It's the last, best shot we have. If this doesn't work, there's nothing else. Everyone braces for the bumps as I lift my foot off the brake and let the car roll to the side of the road.

I exhale deeply and lightly press down on the gas pedal. We start to pick up speed down the gentle slope at the side of the road. Even at that modest speed, no faster than a sprint, my car hits the farmer's field hard. The suspension quakes with every rut in the soil, but I hit the gas harder out of fear that going too slow might get us stuck.

At first, everyone else in the car is just as scared as I am. Olivia clutches Ezra's knee every time the bottom of the car bangs against the ground, and Sam, who hasn't stopped smiling since this morning, is holding onto his margarine container for dear life. The inside of the car turns into a tumble dryer and our loose supplies suffer a serious jostling. Metal rattles, groans, and shakes, setting my teeth on edge, but we're in the thick of it now. I can't stop.

"I immediately regret this decision!" shouts Olivia.

"Oh, come on! It's not that bad," Ezra assures her. I hear the click of a seat-beat unbuckling. "It's actually kinda fun!"

In the rearview mirror, I can see Ezra's head bobbing up and down in perfect harmony with every bump we hit. Sam turns around and starts to laugh, but I can tell he's too nervous to follow suit. Ezra helps Olivia unbuckle her belt and before I know it, they're both bouncing around like a couple of kids at the back of a school bus.

Soon enough, we're all cheering and hollering as we bound through the field, leaving traffic hell in our dust. Things are looking up. I'll be in Alice's arms in no time.

******

I stare at the tangle of tubes and wires under my hood as smoke funnels out from what I assume is the engine. In that moment, I regret not taking shop class, as I have no clue what I'm looking at. Ezra scratches his head and leans in to poke at something, but quickly retracts his hand. He sucks his burnt thumb quietly in defeat.

We're stranded in the middle of a field on a cold March afternoon. My rust bucket of a car is totaled. We're still hours away from our destination. It has been about eight minutes since we left the road on our genius expedition. Civilization is nowhere in sight. We're screwed.

"Well, that was fun," Olivia mutters. "Now what?"

My car sputters one last time before grinding to a loud, unflattering demise.

"Told you this was a bad idea," Sam says.

I punch him hard in the shoulder.

Tip #7: This day will take everything from you. Never forget that.

17 Hours Remaining

"**We Hijack Someone's Car.**"

That is Sam's first suggestion of how to get out of our predicament. Not some last ditch effort after exhausting all possible trains of thought. *First* suggestion.

"You're just full of bad ideas today," I groan.

We've been walking for a while, and haven't even found our way back to the road. The mist makes it impossible to know which way we came in from or which way to go, and Olivia's GPS isn't picking up a location this far out. And time won't pause just because we're lost.

"You got a better one?" Sam asks. "Last I checked we still have hundreds of kilometers to go and a black hole breathing down our necks."

"Not a black hole," Ezra mutters.

"Unless one of you can fly," Sam continues, "that's our best bet. We find a road, flag someone down, and take their car."

"How?" Ezra asks.

Sam pats the holster under his shirt and I hear the gun clink.

"Absolutely not," Olivia says. "If we steal someone's car, we take away their chance to get where they need to go. A stranger shouldn't pay for our mistake. We're not hijacking anything."

I know Sam is thinking in drastic measures for my sake, but his headspace worries me. Yes, I want to get to Alice more than I've ever wanted anything, but is it worth taking someone else's life for?

"Why don't we just go back to the road we were on and ask someone for a ride?" Ezra suggests.

"Because even on the off-chance they *are* going to Wasaga, which is doubtful, we'll *still* be stuck in traffic with the rest of them," Sam says. "Now, if we *take* their car—"

"Stop."

This ethics debate is leading us further away from the point. I need us to focus back on track.

"How close did this little short-cut get us to Wasaga?" I ask. "Before my car decided to explode."

Olivia doesn't check her phone. She bites her lip and keeps her eyes on Sam, looking like she wants to keep fighting to avoid talking to me. Her hesitation makes my mouth dry, my head light, the same nauseating sensation I get moments before vomiting.

"Before we went off the road," she says quietly, "the GPS said we were an hour away by car. On foot, it's…"

"It's what?"

Olivia's eyes fall to the ground. She can't even bear to look at me.

"Too far. We'll get there by morning, but no way there's enough time to turn around and make it to Toronto. Even if you skipped Wasaga and went straight there, you wouldn't even make it halfway. Not on foot."

Her words hit me like a punch to the gut I should have seen coming. Every fear that nagged at me back when Olivia and Ezra first asked to tag along comes out to play. I was naïve, foolish to think that I could make it to the beach and Alice in time. In trying to do both, it was now a very real possibility that neither would happen. And it was all my fault. I was going to let everyone down.

"Well," Sam says. With a bitter smile, he holds out his hand for Ezra to shake. "I guess this is where we say good-bye then."

Ezra stares at Sam's hand, completely bewildered.

"What?"

"The plan was to get Nate to Ali, no matter what," he explains plainly. "Nothing gets in the way of that."

I think maybe Sam's joking, but he's holding off on the punchline way too long.

"The plan was we stick together until Wasaga," Olivia says.

"We can't do both, you said it yourself." Sam's right. There's two roads now. Once we pick one, there's no going back for the other. Not picking one is just a waste of time. "Unless you loosen your rules on stealing cars, I don't see what other options we have."

"We're not stealing anyone's car, Sam." Olivia grits her teeth. That's not a good sign. "It's selfish. Drop it."

"Selfish, huh?" Sam crosses his arms and smirks. That's an even worse sign. "Funny, coming from you."

Ezra steps between Olivia and Sam. My friends are going to tear each other apart unless I do something.

"You two're putting our plan at risk to get to some stupid

beach when you already have each other, right now," Sam says. "Why isn't that enough? Why can't some farmer's field, right here, be a good spot to die? Nate is barely going to have a moment with the girl of his dreams and you two are complaining about a little patch of sand."

"It's more than that, Sam," Ezra snaps back. His face is red, veins in his neck popping. I've never seen him lose his cool like this. "We were going to get married there. I pictured it so clear: Olivia, standing in the sand with waves behind her…I haven't gone a god damn hour since we met without thinking about that day, a day that isn't coming anymore. It might not mean much to you, but it's *everything* to me. You…you wouldn't understand."

Sam launches into a laughing fit, but it's too outlandish to be natural, very Joker-esque.

"Oh, I wouldn't *understand*," he says, drawing out the word like it was a pun. "I see. Why's that? Because Sam's just the fifth wheel? He's the guy who stands on the sidelines while everyone else gets their happy endings? I couldn't *possibly* understand all this love crap the rest of you are so caught up in, could I?"

The outburst has winded him, leaving Sam seething in anger. He's not going to budge, but neither is Ezra. It's like they don't care how badly they wound each other.

"Fuck you, man," Sam growls. "I understand just fine. Nathaniel meets Alice. End of story."

Ezra is going to say something back, then Sam will get madder, and maybe they'll start throwing punches. They'll go back and forth, getting nowhere, until the sky collapses right onto their heads, all because I was waiting for a stupid 'perfect moment'– because I wasn't brave enough to do something until the end of the world. I can't bear to see my friends fight for me anymore. It's time to pick a path.

"This isn't your call," Ezra starts to say. "This—"

"We're going to the beach," I say firmly.

Sam and Ezra turn to me, the heat from their argument instantly deflating. Their expressions are *exactly* the same, down to their eyebrows twitching in sync. It almost makes me laugh, but when I look to Ezra, clutching the collar of my borrowed shirt, I remember our conversation this morning in my bedroom and him asking, 'Are you sure this is what you want?'

"What?" Sam asks.

Alice's face flashes in my mind, the one I first saw of her on my little phone screen. I'll never see that beautiful smile in person. I'll never know what her voice sounds like in my ear. I'll never feel her hand in mine. Time to start rationalizing away the last hope I'll ever have, the last dream I'll never see come true.

"Think about how long it took just to get here," I say. The words fall into place before me like a brick road, perfectly aligned. It's so easy to lie away your aspirations. "Who says it'll be any better once we hit the big city? It'll probably be worse, actually. There's no guarantee I'll make it to…" I pause and sidestep her name. "*Her*, in time, but if we can get to the beach on foot, even if it takes until morning…" I turn to Olivia and Ezra. "In the end, at least you'll get where you belong. And I'll be with my best friends. That's not such a bad way to go."

I put on a brave face and smile to make it seem like this is exactly what I want, but it takes everything I have, maybe even more than what I have, not to break down and cry. That perfect moment alone with Alice, the girl of my dreams, erased, along with the rest of my future.

"She's just an idea," I whisper. "A dream."

Olivia can probably tell that I'm struggling. She comes over, lip trembling, and gives me a long hug. It feels good to be in the arms of a friend at the end of the world. Behind her, I see that Ezra is at a loss. But nowhere is my decision more plainly rejected than on Sam's tightly wound face. Jaw clenched, lips thin, he looks completely betrayed by my choice.

"Nate," Sam whispers. "You're just gonna let her go? After everything? This is what you want?"

Choosing between my friends and Alice is the absolute last thing I ever wanted. But lamenting the loss of something I never had only serves to waste more time. I grab my backpack off the ground, pick a meaningless direction into the mist, and start walking. If I'm forfeiting my final wish, we're making it to that god-damn beach if it's the last thing I do, which it will be.

"Let's get going," I say. "Long walk ahead."

My friends are slow to follow. In fact, I don't hear their footsteps trudging through the soil at all. I turn and find them far away, silhouettes half-hidden in the mist.

"Shouldn't you call Alice?" Olivia calls out. "Tell her what's happening?"

A sickening shudder pulses through me. I don't have the strength in me to pull off a conversation like that. Not yet. I think of how I felt when my mom called to tell me I'd never see her again, and how quickly my world was ripped away from me; that shattered feeling of someone you thought would always being there, someone you loved, being taken away forever. Leaving her hanging is horrible, but is it less horrible than telling her the truth?

"Just let her think I'm coming a little longer," I say. "Hope is a terrible thing to take away. Now come on. No more stops, remember?"

My silhouetted friends pause for one moment longer before gathering their things and emerging back into my sights. They still look confused, but more resigned to the new plan. We took everything we could carry before leaving my car behind, so we're well-stocked for the hike. I'm travelling pretty light, with only a few snacks and my phone charger stuffed into my backpack, though without a car, the charger is useless. I check my phone. Three-quarters battery. If it dies before I find an outlet, it's truly over. I will be forever lost to Alice, and she will be lost to me.

Sam's sideways glances make me feel even worse. He's looking for an explanation, I know it. I give him the best I've got, but it barely makes sense to me.

"I waited too long to meet her," I say, defeated. "This is the last day and…" It's such a terrible thought I barely have the courage to voice it. "And I wasted our time, chasing after someone who will never be real."

Sam scowls at me, the kind the old Sam—the Sam I knew before today—wore all the time. In that scowl, I realize I've taken something from him too; his shot to be a part of something good for once.

"I just can't believe you're doing this." He sounds so disappointed, like a brother who expects better. "I know how you feel about her. Everyone does. I've seen the way your dopey face lights up every time she sent you a message. I've had to endure all the sappy metaphors and cheesy poems you two have made in each other's honour. I wouldn't have agreed to this little trip…if I thought it was a waste." He stops himself. The level of his sincerity disarms me. Some sad desperation in Sam's eyes tells me that he needed this just as much as me, and in that moment, I feel that he believed in me more than I did. "She's not just a dream. This was your shot at something real. I didn't think you'd give up so easily."

His words cut just as deep as I expected them too. Who needs a guilty conscience when you have a friend as good as Sam?

"We all have to make sacrifices today," I tell him.

"I think you made one too many."

"Guys!" Olivia shouts from up ahead. "Come look!"

I can see the silhouettes of the two giants in the mist up ahead. They've come to a stop. Sam and I hustle to reunite with our friends, but before we even arrive, my heart starts to pound for a reason I can't explain. Maybe some part of me thinks, naively, there's still a chance. Maybe we made it further than we thought. The mist peels back as we draw near, and their discovery is made known.

A quiet, empty road. Not a soul in either direction. Next to the road is a big green sign. 'Wasaga Beach – 60km.' That's it, the dreadful confirmation that there really is no hope of reaching both destinations. The path to Alice disappears behind me, lost to the mist.

My phone vibrates, but I don't get the same thrill I used to from seeing her name. In fact, I don't feel anything. The message feels like it's for another person.

➢ Alice: *From our thirty-second conversation, I can confirm that your friends are everything you said they were. You're in good company, Nathaniel :) Guess I'll be a part of that company soon, huh?*

She has no idea.

Tip #8: Love means doing whatever it takes. Do whatever it takes.

14 Hours Remaining

I'm watching the sun go down, knowing full well that it will only come up again one more time. The mist is gone, but the road just keeps stretching out forever. My feet move beneath me, taking me in one direction, but it's like I'm not even connected to them. My whole body is wrapped in some kind of stasis that lets me move, but experience nothing. This is what waiting feels like at the end of the world. Waiting is poison, slowly killing time that could have been spent doing something beautiful.

Standing in pairs on each side of the road, we wait for someone to pick us up. Ezra and Olivia have been quietly discussing something for a while, but I can't hear them over Sam's constant social media updates. I just keep my thumb out like a hitchhiker in an old movie. I would dive in front of a moving vehicle if that's what it took. Any minute now, I keep telling myself. Any minute now, someone would come roaring up that road and save us from this purgatory. Any minute.

I stopped checking my phone a little while ago. It vibrates from time to time, but I just kick at the crumbling concrete that makes up this forgotten road. Alice is texting me, I know it, probably checking for updates, but I can't bear to watch my battery drain. She wants to know if I'm okay, but I don't have the heart to tell her I'm not going to make it. I've edited and rephrased it a million different ways in my head, but it never comes together right. It sounds like the most awful thing anyone has ever said, every time.

Sam can see my despair and tries to cheer me up.

"Oh, goodie," he says, once again scrolling through his phone. "Government secrets are starting to leak all over the web, because why the fuck not at this point. Apparently the Illuminati are real and they control basically everything."

"What an earth-shaking shock," Olivia quips. "Let me guess, the government taps all our phones and computers, too?"

"Obviously," Sam replies. "But we've known that for years. No clue how I'm not in jail with what's on my hard-drive. Oh, and all celebrities are lizard people in human costumes."

"Really?" Ezra asks.

"No, but the day's not over yet. It could still happen."

Sam looks to me, hopeful, like a comedian who wants someone to critique his latest set. I've got nothing to give him. I just look down at my feet, and watch them move on their own. I wonder what Alice is thinking right now. Maybe she can feel that I've already let her go. She has her family, I tell myself. She's with people she loves, people who have loved her since birth. I'm just a guy she almost met. People lose out on that all the time.

Then I picture that mysterious present she said she made for me, wrapped in a nice little bow I'll never open.

"Your phone's buzzing like crazy."

I hadn't noticed, but Sam and Olivia switched places when I wasn't looking, like ninja tag-team partners. Sam's brand of humour hadn't worked on me, so they throw in the best friend to turn my frown upside-down, huh? Sneaky beavers.

"There's a little building up ahead," Olivia says, pointing up the road. I can see it. Looks like a small rest-stop for people who couldn't quite keep their bladders under control until Wasaga. Behind the building are the skeletal remains of a forest whose trees hadn't gotten the chance to grow back their leaves. Beach must still be a ways off. "Bet you can charge your phone there."

"What's the point?" I ask. My voice sounds so small, like the volume is barely above mute. "I can't tell her. With my mom it was like…there was no time. It just happened, like a car crash. Didn't see it coming until she was gone. This just sits still, pressing down on me. I'm stuck, and every move feels like the wrong one. I just…I just wanted to see her face. I'm sorry."

I don't know why I apologized. I always do when I cry. It feels like I'm putting the other person out when I break down like this. Olivia knows how to handle it better than anyone else. She wraps her arm around my shoulder and pulls me in close to hide my tears from the rest of the world. That's the part I expect, the comfort that comes from a best friend.

I don't expect her to whisper in my ear.

"Call her. Right now. I have a story to tell."

Call her? I pull back to read her expression. She's completely serious, maybe even a little playful, like she has a secret. Usually I can take a stab at what's going on in Olivia's head and get it right, but I'm as lost as I was back in the mist.

"What?" I ask. I look across the road to find Ezra wearing a knowing smile. Sam looks as confused as I am which makes me feel a little less stupid. Or maybe more stupid. "Olivia, I don't—"

"We told Alice that we'd share the story of how we met," Ezra says, crossing the empty road to stand next to his giantess. They share a look, one I can only define as melancholic. There's definitely something going on between them, but I'm not getting it. "We wouldn't want to let down the girl of your dreams. What kind of friends would do that?"

"No offense," Sam says, butting in. "But is now really the best time?"

"Now is really all we've got," Olivia says. That's not the first time she's said that today. It's starting to grow on me. She turns to me, her eyes beckoning. "Please, call her."

Why is this suddenly so important? Whatever game she's playing, I don't know the rules, how to win, or if it's even a game, but I'm too tired and defeated to really argue with her. After all, it will be nice to hear Alice's voice again. It will be awful to tell her that we'll be nothing more; nothing more to each other than words on a screen.

Before I make the call, I check my battery. No matter how long we talk, this will drain my phone to near-death. If this rest-stop up ahead does have an outlet, I'll be sitting there quite a while charging it back up, or I'll have to resort to Sam's as a back-up. That's if Alice even wants to talk to me again after I drop the motherlode of all bad news, death by black hole notwithstanding.

Alice picks up on the first ring.

"Didn't expect to hear from you so soon!" she says. The joy in his voice physically pains me. It's like putting down a puppy. "I mean, I was texting, but I figured you guys were driving. Did you make it to the beach already?"

I shake my head, open and close my mouth at least three times without saying anything. How did my mom do it? How did she say good-bye, knowing it was for the last time? She was so much braver than me. I look to my friends for guidance, courage, to throw me a lifeboat and help me from drowning.

"Alice," I say quietly. "About the beach. I…I can't. We—"

"We couldn't wait to tell you," Olivia says, stepping in and taking the phone from my hand. "I seem to remember Ezra and I promising you the story of how we met, isn't that right?"

"This is gonna be embarrassing," Sam says excitedly. "I can already tell. Wait!"

He rips open his backpack and fishes out a pack of M&Ms. He pops one in his mouth and leans back, ready for a show.

"Continue," he says with his mouth full.

"Well, the end of the world has a way of accelerating plans," Olivia explains. "We may never meet, but we owe you this one."

Olivia hands the phone back to me and takes a quiet, introspective moment to herself, like an actor remembering her lines. She nods and gestures for Ezra to begin. Something is eating away at his thoughts, I can tell, but Ezra does his best to focus on the task at hand.

"Fancy meeting you here," Olivia says with a curtsy. "Poor Boy."

"Tall Girl," Ezra replies with a reluctant bow.

They're using their pet names. Without the rum and coke in my system, it just sounds weird.

"How long has it been?"

"We were both in grade six, so we must've been like twelve."

"*I* was twelve. You were still eleven, Mr. Late Birthday."

"You cougar."

"What can I say? I like 'em young."

"I was sitting at the beach in Wasaga." Ezra paces around a little and takes a seat on the side of the road when he finds the perfect spot. "Here, looking out on the lake, feeling sorry for myself, when you came up and said—"

******

"You're that poor boy everyone makes fun of."

On that sunny day at Wasaga Beach, young children frolicked through the sand and splashed water at their friends. The bus driver read a newspaper in the parking lot, away from the noise he would soon endure on the return trip. Mrs. O'Hagan--

"Are you sure it was Mrs. O 'Hagan's class?" Ezra asks, interrupting the story. "I thought it was Bolton's?"

"Bolton taught comm-tech," Olivia replies. "Why on Earth would he take us to the beach?"

Ezra thought for a moment.

"Fair point. Continue."

Mrs. O'Hagan, the teacher in charge of this fateful school trip, multi-tasked between working on her tan and ensuring nobody drowned.

But that was all rather superfluous to the scene that unfolded away from the crowd between a nosy young girl and a moody boy who was just trying to be left alone.

"I was not being moody," Ezra mutters.

"Oh, I'm sorry, are you telling the story, or am I?" Olivia asks. Ezra gestures for her to keep going. "Thank you."

The 'Poor Boy' looked up with a tired disdain at the girl.

"You're that tall girl everyone makes fun of," he shot back.

"Yep," she replied plainly.

Poor Boy had meant the insult to inflict pain the same way his distasteful moniker hurt him, but the name 'Tall Girl' rolled right off her back like rain. This softened him to her.

"I'm just a poor boy," *he sang to himself.* "I need no sympathy."

"What's that?" *Tall Girl asked.*

"A song my parents listen to sometimes."

"Cool. What does it mean?"

"Don't know. It's a weird song. I kinda like it, I guess."

"Can you sing it for me?"

"No."

A long, awkward pause ensued. Tall Girl twisted her hair into braids while Poor Boy picked at his shoelaces. For a moment, it looked like their encounter had met a swift, unsatisfying end. For many, that would have been it. But Tall Girl had different plans. Her eyes lit up with an idea.

"You wanna go on a date?" *she asked.*

Poor Boy physically recoiled from the notion.

"What!" *he shrieked.*

"A date," *she repeated.* "You wanna go on one with me?"

Poor Boy couldn't believe his ears. He scanned the area, probably to make sure no one was listening in. There could be no witnesses to this blasphemous insanity.

"Uh, whuh, guh." *He stuttered and stammered until the word finally came to him.* "When?"

"Now," Tall Girl replied.

Poor Boy took a deep breath and gulped nervously, like he was about to dive off the cliff at the far end of the beach. He wiped off the sand stuck to the palms of his hand and stood uncomfortable next to this strange girl he had seen many times before in class, but had never really noticed until now. She had pretty hair. Even her braces weren't that bad to look at.

"I actually kind of liked the braces," Ezra adds.

"Uh, okay," he said.

Tall Girl was very pleased, but she, like he, had never done this before. They walked along the shoreline, saying nothing, and avoiding eye contact. Another prolonged pause threatened to kill the momentum of the moment. Some couples speak of sparks flying upon their first encounter. This was not the case for young Olivia and Ezra.

"What do we do?"

Tall Girl thought upon this and drew upon her wealth of second-hand knowledge on the subject of fine dating.

"Walk around, hold hands, talk about stuff," she said.

"Do we have to hold hands?"

"I think so. That's what my parents did, before my mom left, and people in movies."

"Oh."

This is how their first conversation went, with fits and starts, like a sputtering engine that would almost find its rhythm right before dying all over again. Pulling teeth was quicker, and easier to watch.

"Do you like movies?" Tall Girl asked.

"I like music," Poor Boy replied.

"Movies have music."

For no apparent reason, in a move that could only be described as courage in the extreme or brazen irrationality, Poor Boy gracelessly attempted to hold Tall Girl's hand, despite his own earlier protests. It was a gutsy move—borderline lunacy—but magically, it paid off. Tall Girl didn't retract her hand in horror. Instead, she held on.

"Your hands are soft," Poor Boy muttered.

"Do you like that?" Tall Girl asked, showing off her steel smile.

"Sure."

Poor Boy rallied his nerves and did something the history books could only describe as the single greatest act of bravery ever known: He lifted his head and met love eye to eye. There was no shame, no judgement. He knew her, and she knew him. It happened in an instant, but there was no going back from there.

Just as those two young souls began to intertwine, a chill shot up Poor Boy's spine. From the corner of his eye, an intruder spawned from nowhere. He tried to pull his hand away, but it was too late. The damage had been done.

The intruder was a young boy named Travis and he wasn't about to keep what he had seen a secret. Laughing maniacally, he called out to the entire beach.

"Hey, look everyone!" he squealed. "Braceface found herself a boooooyfriend!"

Humiliated, Poor Boy tried to retreat, but Tall Girl held on.

"Eat an ass, Travis!" she shouted. "Next time you cry during Sunday mass, maybe I won't keep it a secret!"

Travis' face burned bright red.

"It was a beautiful service!" he barked back. "You said you wouldn't tell anyone!"

"Oops!"

"I'm telling Mrs. O'Hagan you swore!"

"Go tell, bitch!"

"Ha!" Sam laughs, mouth-filled with chocolate. "Get wrecked Travis. Idiot."

Positively fuming, Travis ran off to tattle his little tale. Baring her armored teeth and with her hands balled into fists, Tall Girl looked ready to chase him down and pummel him into the ground. Remembering that she was supposed to be on a date, she gathered her composure and feigned a lady-like demeanor.

"Sorry," she whispered. "My dad says I need to work on my anger."

"That was awesome," Poor Boy said.

Tall Girl was caught off-guard, but nonetheless pleased. She dropped the act and spared another one of her steel smiles. Poor Boy did something he hadn't done in a long time: He smiled back.

"And that's when I knew," Ezra says.

"Knew what?" Olivia asks.

"That I'd never feel sorry for myself again, that I'd always have someone to protect me, because I had you."

Ezra fumbles with something in his pocket. It's a cool March evening, but there is a layer of perspiration glistening upon his forehead. I look to Sam to see if he is picking up the same signs I am. His M & M munching slows to a crawl.

"And if you, Olivia Meyers, AKA Tall Girl, would do me, Ezra Jones, AKA Poor Boy, the honor…" He gets down on one knee and does something the history books can only describe as the single greatest act of bravery ever known. "I'd like to have you for the rest of my life. Will you marry me?"

Total silence, interrupted only by the wind and Sam biting down on a particularly loud piece of candy.

"Whaaat the fuck just happened?"

From his pocket, Ezra takes out a ring made of grass and offers it up to Olivia. Her hands clasp over her mouth and tears flood her eyes.

"I know it's not a real ring," Ezra explains. "And I know we're not on the beach, but Sam was right. I don't care if we're at Wasaga, or if this is our last day on Earth. The truth, Olivia, is that I've wanted to do this since the first moment we met."

Olivia, like the rest of us, is too stunned to give an immediate response. An awkward silence, not unlike the ones described in the story of how Olivia and Ezra met, ensues. On the other end of the phone, Alice is understandably even more confused.

"Did Ezra just propose?" she asks.

"Yes, he did," I reply.

"Well, what did she say?"

I wait for the scene to play out so I can give an accurate report. Ezra shifts around on his knee, as the side of the road doesn't really offer a comfortable kneeling position. Olivia shakes her head and wipes her eyes dry. She clears her throat and tries to give her answer, but starts crying again, which turns to an incredulous laugh.

"Yes," she finally says. "Yes, of course! Sorry that took so long to get out. I'm all choked up."

A wave of joy washes over Ezra. He puts the grass ring on her finger and clumsily stands for that fabled kiss all good love stories end on.

"Yes," I tell Alice. "She said yes."

I look to my left and find Sam wiping a tear from his cheek. He looks at me, slightly embarrassed.

"Damn, he's good," he mutters. "Even I would have said yes to that."

A quick, high-pitched beep emits from my phone. I turn the screen around to confirm what I already know. Dead. With all the commotion from the proposal, I totally forgot to tell Alice about the 'slight' change in plans. I'd get it over with the second my phone was charged, I told myself. If Ezra can propose to Olivia, I can tell Alice I'm not coming. No more putting it off. I owe her.

Sam and I congratulate the 'bride and groom.' I can't remember ever seeing Olivia so happy, not even as kids. Ezra looks ready to run a marathon with all the pent-up energy coursing through him. He plants another huge kiss on her lips.

"We might be the world's last newlyweds," he says.

My friends laugh, and I do too, but only for appearances. I will never have the history of these two giants. Not with Alice, not with anyone. There won't be a 'beach-moment' for me or waxing nostalgic for the first time I ever met the girl of my dreams. It's petty to be jealous at a time like this, I know, but it hurts just the same.

Ezra looks at Olivia for a long time, and that melancholic look returns. They nod to each other.

"Man, I've gotta hit the bathroom after that," Ezra says. "Proposing really makes you have to pee."

"Dude, TMI," Sam says.

Ezra laughs at Sam's 'joke' a little harder than is warranted. He gives me a firm hug and sprints off toward the rest-stop. The rest of us take a little more time walking over. Olivia shows off the ring on her finger like it's made of 24 karat grass.

"I was worried he wouldn't know my size," she jokes.

"Did you have any idea?" I ask. "That he would propose, I mean."

"It's the end of the world," she says with a sly smile. "If he didn't make a move, I would have."

We arrive at the rest-stop and I dart inside to look for an outlet. There's one right beside the sink. I carefully teeter my phone on the ledge and let it charge. Due to the disgusting smell coming from every corner of the guy's washroom, and some stains I don't want to know the origins of, waiting outside is pretty much my only option.

It's then, when I return, that I notice Olivia won't stop looking at me. Maybe she feels guilty about everything. She shouldn't. This is her last day as much as it is mine. I want to tell her that, but I don't know how to bring it up. She cuts through the awkward silence.

"Actually, I might as well use the bathroom while we're here," she says. She walks toward the ladies' side of the rest-stop with measured steps. Olivia stops, still in view, and turns to us. "Guys?"

"Yeah?" Sam replies.

"I'm really glad you were there for all that," she says,

smiling. "Today wouldn't have been the same without you, both. Thank you. For everything."

I imagine I'd become pretty sentimental the day I became a fiancé too, so I let the strange comment slide.

"You're welcome," I say.

"Weird thing to say before going to the bathroom," Sam adds.

Olivia laughs a little, bows her head, and enters the bathroom, out of sight. The moment she leaves, Sam sighs heavily and throws his backpack to the ground.

"I wish this had been enough for us," he growls.

"What do you mean?" I ask.

"Rings made of grass. Friends. I wish this had been enough. Why'd we have to go chasing God particles?"

"You mean the scientists?" I ask.

"Yeah. If it weren't for those assholes, Ezra would have been able to propose on his own time, at the beach like he wanted. Olivia would be thinking about dresses and all that shit. You could have…met Alice."

He's pissed, and I'm a little surprised. This is a different tune than the one he'd been singing earlier this morning.

"I thought today was a blank slate? You said it was wiping everything clean."

"Maybe some things deserved to stick."

"And what about you?" I ask.

"What about me?"

"What would you get up to if this wasn't the end?"

"I honestly never thought about it, but after today… I'd stop waiting for something to happen. I'd do something. I'm not sure what the hell it would be, but it would be *something*. I'd take what's mine."

Sam looks up at the sun. We watch that great ball of fire fall into the horizon one last time. As far as finales go, it is breath-taking, even if for the simple, overwhelming fact that something that had happened billions of times before wouldn't happen tomorrow, or ever again. Would our beloved sun even notice we were gone?

Maybe it did know or maybe I never really took the time to count how long a sunset was, because on this day, our sun lingers longer in the sky than I have ever known, like a friend who hates good-byes.

Good-byes…

"The hell is taking them so long?" Sam asks.

I immediately feel incredibly stupid. Perhaps it was the loss of Alice, or the suddenness of Ezra's proposal, but the past hour, which had felt like gentle waves lapping at my ankles, has risen to a tidal wave, knocking me on my ass. How could this blind-side me?

I rush from Sam's side into the men's rest-stop calling Ezra's name. I check every stall, but the place is empty. This can't be happening. Forgoing all etiquette, I barge into the ladies' bathroom calling out Olivia, then Ezra again, anyone that can hear me. I run back into the mens' room, thinking somehow, I missed a hiding place, but no. The place is empty.

"Olivia!" I call out. "Ezra! Don't you fucking do this!"

Sam runs to my side, gun withdrawn, spinning around to see what all the commotion is about.

"What's going on?" he asks. "Where are they?"

I fall to my knees and think back to that melancholic look they gave each other, the way Ezra hugged me, the look Olivia was giving me. Those best friends of mine…

I look up to Sam with tears in my eyes, and find him looking over to the sink where I had placed my phone to charge. Two other phones lay next to it; Ezra and Olivia's phones, left behind.

I pull myself off the bathroom floor and hunch over the sink. Olivia's phone is on, her screen open to a long, typed message. The note starts with two words, 'We're sorry,' and I don't know if I can bring myself to read the rest.

Sam puts the gun away and rests his hand on my back.

"What does it say?" he asks.

I have to wipe the tears from my eyes to see the screen clearly. Every word is a road bump, lodged in my throat and threatening to break into a flood of sobs. But I hold it all down and read my best friends' good-bye.

We're sorry. We wanted to leave some other way, but like everything today, we do the best with the time we're given. I wanted to drag this out, have a big group cry, but Ezra was right. If we're to give you any chance to reach Alice in time, it had to be quick. Like Ezra said this morning, whatever it takes, right? That's why we didn't tell you and why we left our phones behind. Not just so you can have back-ups for when yours die, but so that you don't try to call or come after us. Knowing you would do anything for Ezra and me is enough. Don't come looking for us. We don't want you to sacrifice any more than you already have for our sake. You're my best friend, Nate. I've always known that, and I'll know it at the end. I don't need you to be here. All I want is for you to be happy. Sam, take care of him and try not to get into too much trouble. I guess we'll have to live with the mystery of the margarine container (but not for long, haha). Nathaniel, Alice, you two. When this world goes dark, hold on to each other. Right to the very end. We will both miss you all so much. No matter what happens, I hope we all end up in the same place.

#Seeyouontheotherside

Love your friends,
Ezra and Olive

P.S. I came back to change her name lol – Ezra

The phone slides from my hand when I finish reading it, like sand through my fingers. How could they have slipped away so easily? A panicked instinct takes over and my mind is resolved before I even rise to my feet.

"We have to find them," I say, heading for the exit.

Sam catches my hand and stops me. He looks sad, but the bitterness is gone again. There's a determination in his eyes, like when he told me he was coming with me this morning.

"Nate, they could be anywhere by now," he says. "We've gotta let them go."

I pull my hand away.

"So we look everywhere! They can't have gone far. Think about it. They're probably--"

"You read the note. They don't want to be found. They want us to keep going. They want the same thing I do; for you to reach Alice."

Before this moment, I thought it impossible to be excited and sad at the same time, but I seem to have struck that perfect equilibrium. How can my best friends' departure cause a surge of hope? Should I feel awful about that? I've never felt so torn in my whole life.

"How...how could they?" I stutter and sob. "They...they didn't even say good-bye."

Sam pulls me in close to console me. It's not the same comfort as Olivia offered, but realizing that he is now the last person on this planet I may ever hold gives another kind of comfort. He's all I've got.

"They did," he whispers. "And they gave us a chance. We have to make the most of it."

Slowly, I come around to the reality of the situation. Two of my best friends, Olivia and Ezra, are gone. They left so I can go back in time and pick another path, the one I thought erased. That perfect moment with the girl of my dreams was once again open to me. We couldn't waste another moment.

"Okay," I say, pulling away from Sam. After a few deep breaths, I collect the phones off the sink ledge and stuff them into my pockets. "Okay. What's the plan?" Before Sam even opens his mouth I can tell where the conversation is steering. "And just because Olivia's gone, doesn't mean we're stealing—"

"Nate, I'm telling you, we will *not* make it unless we get a car," Sam says. "I don't see Oprah around giving out free ones. There's no way around it. Either we take one, or we don't make it, and then Olivia and Ezra left us for nothing."

With Olivia gone, the coalition of ethics between our friend group is significantly weakened, and with time ticking down, the bar of what's 'right' is getting awfully low in my mind. But I want ground rules before things get taken too far.

"Fine," I say. Sam fist pumps the air. "But! We find a *parked* car, one that looks abandoned. And the gun never comes out, for any reason. No one gets hurt."

Sam makes no effort to hide his dissatisfaction, but grunts his agreement to my terms anyway. As much as I'll miss Ezra and Olivia, it's much easier to be on the same page with only two people. We have a plan. We have a chance.

Sam and I fly out of the pungent rest-stop likes bats out of hell. Truth be told, I can't get out of there fast enough, but something brings me to a halt right outside. I turn to face the skeletal forest and look deep within. Somewhere in there, two giants in love stomp across the forest floor, heading to the spot where they first met many years ago. I won't be there, but in my mind, there is no better ending for Ezra and Olivia.

In half a day's time, the world would be undone. All its sights and mysteries and memories will be lost. But right now, basking in the glow of our planet's final golden hour, that moment seems so far away. It feels like a crowning achievement, just to be a part of something so beautiful. I'm sure wherever my friends are they see the same thing I do.

Tip #9: Your hands are going to get dirty. Bring sanitizer

11 Hours Remaining

"I can't wait for you to meet her, Sam."

I must have said it like fifty times since our course correction, but I can't stop myself. There's so much pent-up, giddy excitement in me that certain things that should matter—like the fact that we've been searching for an abandoned car far longer than I'd hoped—don't faze me in the least.

"I can't wait for you to stop saying that," Sam says. He points to a sign that mentions an on-route up ahead with a gas station and a few fast-food restaurants. We have our heading. "We should be careful of the night."

"Why's that?"

"Won't see the black hole coming if it gets here early. Just keep looking at the stars until the sun comes back."

The next time we see the sun will be the last. Like a flare, it will rise into the sky, warning us of what's waiting on the other end of the horizon. For now, the burgeoning night serves as a prelude to that unending darkness. Sam and I rely on our cell phones and the occasional street light to guide our way. Without Olivia and Ezra, the world seems quieter.

"So what do you think we'll do when we get to Alice?" Sam asks. "Does she have an Xbox? PS4?"

"We're not playing video games with her, Sam," I say. "I didn't come all this way to play Call of Duty with the girl of my dreams."

"Who said Call of Duty? I was thinking Apex or Street Fighter. If she can't beat me in those, she's probably not good enough for you."

"Because the true measure of a woman's worth is how good she is at video games, right?"

"You got it, brother."

I can see the lights from the on-route well before we arrive. It's the first real sign of civilization we've seen since our unfortunate little short-cut. There's the gas station, which looks empty, and several big bright fast-food logos. Even from a distance I can tell we're in for some slim pickings. There's only a handful of cars scattered around the parking lot. How many of them are abandoned? How many still have keys?

Sam crouches low and uses a ditch for cover, like some secret agent scoping out a meeting spot. I don't see anybody, and refuse to skulk in a dirty ditch.

"Any hostiles?" he asks.

"No, Sam," I groan. "Quit screwing around."

Keeping low, Sam exits the ditch and scurries on toward the on-route parking lot. I chase after him, vigilant of any unexpected movement. As far as I can tell, we're the only ones here. The lights inside the restaurants aren't on, so I can't get a good look inside unless I put my face right up against the glass. An old mini-van is the closest vehicle to us, so we check that one first.

The moment we approach the driver's side, I wish we hadn't.

The man must've died a while ago, maybe as soon as he learned of the world's impending doom. There he sits, in the driver's seat of his car, head tilted to the sky, with a bullet hole under his chin. A circle of blood and gore hang over his head like a halo.

"Why would someone kill themselves?" Sam asks, poking his head through the driver's side window in search of the man's gun. The body doesn't seem to have any effect on him. He comes up empty-handed. Stolen already, probably. He finds the keys, though. "Can't they be a little more patient?"

I try to ignore the smell inside the car, but it's enough to make my gag. I can't stop looking at that halo. I can't stop thinking of Dan on the school roof.

"Maybe it's the waiting they can't stand," I whisper, my teeth chattering from the cold. "I'm not getting in that car."

"Yeah, you're right, we should leave the poor soul alone," Sam says, tossing the keys back into the dead man's lap. "Come on. More cars to check. Can't lose hope after one dead guy."

Sam steps away from the mini-van, giving me a clear view at the man inside. He's alone, not even an open cell-phone in his lap or hand. I don't have to wonder very hard at what drove him to do this. A silly thought pops into my mind: I wish I could have been there for him. Maybe me just being there would have helped.

I turn away from the man to find Sam, eyes as big as spotlights, pointing straight at a shiny, silver Corvette. It's an older model, the kind my dad would have marveled over. Sam scans the parking lot one last time before casually approaching the abandoned vehicle. He runs his finger along the driver's side door and gives it a solid punch. No alarm. No witnesses.

The windows are already down, and the roof is off, so we don't have to smash anything to get inside. It's like it's waiting for us to take it.

No matter how empty the parking lot appears, I still feel eyes in the sky, judging me. Stupid Catholic upbringing. With religious paranoia biting at my heels, I hesitantly approach the vehicle and peer inside, hoping the keys are sitting in the ignition. No such luck.

"Hold this for a sec," Sam says.

He hands me his precious margarine container and starts rifling through his bag. The container is light, but there's definitely something inside. I can feel a small weight shifting as I tilt it side to side.

"What's inside this thing, anyway?" I ask, cracking the lid open just a tad.

"*Don't* open that!" Sam yells. He jumps to his feet and snatches the container from my grasp. He clutches it close and inspects the lid, as if something might have gotten loose. He shoots me a betrayed look. "*Please*, don't open it. Hold, don't open."

"All right, jeez. You've been holding it tight all day is all. Won't happen again."

Sam appraises my apology and slowly lowers his guard. Reluctantly, he transfers custody of the margarine container back to me. To put his mind at ease, I show him my fingers; firmly keeping the lid closed.

"It's nothing," he says. "Just…it's nothing."

"Mhm," I grunt. "Sure seems like nothing."

I choose not to pursue an investigation, allowing Sam to concentrate on his nefarious scheme. One way or another, I will get to the bottom of this margarine mystery by the day's end.

A thin strip of metal slips free from the tangled web of junk inside Sam's bag. He slips the metal strip down along the inside of driver's side door, jiggles it around a little, and pop goes the lock on the door. Sam tries the handle, and to my surprise, it opens without a hitch. I might be impressed if it wasn't so illegal, and useless.

"We could have just hopped in," I say. "There's no roof."

"Yeah, but then bringing this would have been pointless," Sam says, putting the metal strip back in his bag.

"Were you planning on stealing a car today?"

"Maybe."

Sam ducks into the driver's seat and reverently wraps his fingers around the steering wheel. A beautiful, fast car like this could cover a lot of ground, quickly. Not a bad ride to roll up to the girl of my dreams, either. Just have to find those pesky keys first.

We toss the interior, flipping down the sun visor mirrors, checking the side door pockets, the dashboard, and even the glove compartment. Nothing. The owners must have taken the keys with them.

"Damn." How many cars were we going to have to break into before we found the one? From the looks of this parking lot, we only have two cars left to check. If neither of them work, how much time would that take to find another parking lot? "Guess we'll have to find another one."

Sam does not share in my disappointment. Instead, he wears a roguish grin.

"You underestimate my power," he says.

He pushes the driver seat back and stoops under the steering wheel. He rips off some paneling and pulls down a handful of wires. I've seen enough movies to know what he's attempting.

"You know how to hotwire a car?" I ask.

"Sure," he replies. "Watched a few Youtube videos, read a few Reddit posts. Practically an expert on the subject. Old 1978 Corvette like this should be a piece of cake."

He tears the plastic coating off one of the wires and gives it a long look that I wouldn't describe as 'confident.'

"Huh," he mutters. "This looks different."

"This isn't going to work, is it?"

"Just keep watch."

I exit the vehicle and stand guard near the driver's side, armed with the margarine container. Not that there's much to stand guard against in this empty patch of pavement. The occasional bird chirps in the night, a squirrel hops along in search of scraps…was that a shadow on the far end of the parking lot?

"Apparently NASA prepared for something like this to happen," Sam calls out. I can hear him still fiddling with the wiring. "Worldwide extinction, I mean. I read that they're launching these time capsules into space, full of stuff from all across human history. Books, pictures, video clips of what we were like. Maybe aliens will find them ages from now and we won't be forgotten. Oh, they even put some DNA samples of us in there. Maybe we'll get cloned! That would be dope."

Sam continues to ramble as I step away from the vehicle to get a better look at the half-imagined shadow. One of the parking lot lighting poles is flickering, and from that sporadic light, I see a figure emerge from the far end. It's a large man, and he's heading our way.

"Shit," I gasp. "Sam someone's coming!"

I retreat back to the car in hope that my warning scares Sam into abandoning his hijacking attempts, but he is undeterred. The man is bigger than Sam and I combined. He sees what we're doing and starts shouting. If we don't leave soon, we risk a confrontation, or worse.

"Sam, we promised—"

"Take my gun," Sam says coolly.

"What?"

Sam takes a break from his wire-fiddling to toss me his gun. I nearly drop the margarine container trying to catch it. The weapon is heavier than I expected, and much more difficult to wield than in video games.

"Let him know we're packing," he says. "If that doesn't scare him off, fire over his head."

This is insane. Surely, he's kidding. I've never shot a gun before, let alone shooting it *at another person*. End of the world or not, this is the kind of shit that gets you to the front of the line at the gates of hell.

The first picture I ever saw of Alice flashes in my mind. Without a ride, whatever afterlife awaited me would be spent cherishing only pictures; pictures, and words on a screen. It's not enough.

With a margarine container in one trembling hand and a

gun in the other, I take aim. Please, I pray, let that be enough to ward this guy away. But he doesn't stop. Maybe he can't see the gun yet, or maybe he has weapons of his own. Was a Corvette really worth a bullet between the eyes?

"Get away from there!" I hear the man shout. "That's mine. If I find one scratch on that car, you're dead. You hear me? Dead!"

I can see him pretty clearly now. Middle-aged, beard, tattoos, muscles. He'd steamroll us without breaking a sweat. A bullet might only make him angrier.

"Sam, we gotta go!" I yell.

"Almost there," he grunts. "So close."

Not close enough. I try to pull him out from under the steering wheel, but he kicks me away. Suddenly, I hear the engine stutter, stall for a moment, and then come roaring back to life. Sam hollers and slaps the steering wheel.

"Get in!" he yells, taking over the driver's seat.

We swore that we wouldn't take someone else's chance, but Sam isn't getting out, and the man is closing in. By the crazed look in his eye I can tell he's not in the mood to negotiate. Words won't calm him down. We've committed to this.

I run to the other side of the car and dive over the passenger side door. Sam slams his foot to the floor just as I get my seatbelt on. The quick jolt of speeds snaps my head back and puts a twinge in my neck, but the car doesn't immediately take off. The engine sputters and the whole car rocks back and forth. Sam fiddles with the wires again, but the man is upon us, and for whatever reason, has decided to come for me.

"Get out of there right now!" he yells, grabbing at my sweater. "I need this car to get home!"

The man tries to lift me out of the car, and if it weren't for the seatbelt locking me in place, he probably could have done it.

The sheer anger in his feral eyes, the strength of his hands on my arms, makes me think I might die right there.

"Go faster!" I shout.

Tiny sparks dance off the wire tips and the engine hums without faltering. Again Sam hits the pedal hard, and this time the car takes off like a rocket. The man makes one last desperate attempt to pull me out, but loses his grip and falls behind the car. Rubber burns in the air as we screech out of the parking lot, leaving the man in a thick cloud made by his stolen car.

I sink into my seat, shaking uncontrollably. My face in the rearview mirror is gaunt, and my stomach feels empty. A light-headed nausea starts to take over, like I might throw up. The window's down, and the cold wind coming in from the night feels so inviting.

I lean my head outside the Corvette and let it all out. Much better.

"I hope you didn't get that on the door," Sam mutters. "Not many car-washes open at this hour."

I don't even know what to say to him. We had a plan, made a promise, and at the first opportunity, Sam threw it all out the window and nearly got us killed. He lied to me.

"What the hell was that about?" I ask.

"What do you mean? I got us a car!" Sam exclaims. "You should be thanking me. I'm partial to bouquets for gifts of gratitude, but a nicely worded card—"

"We promised we wouldn't take from someone else. He said he needed this to get home. What if that man was on his way to his family? What if he won't make it now because of us? We should turn around."

"Uh, absolutely not. You see how pissed he was? Plus, I don't want to drive over your puke on the way back. I'm starting to sense you're not pumped about this."

"You're god-damn right I'm not. We're supposed to be on the same page here. We should have run the second we saw him coming! 'Shoot above his head?' Are you kidding me?"

"Shouldn't use the Lord's name in vain so late in the game."

His aloof attitude causes something inside me to snap. I lash out in a flurry of punches, nothing too hard, but enough to let him know I'm serious.

"What the hell, Nate?" Sam says while trying to keep us on the road. "You saw the dude. He would've eaten us both alive!"

"He had every right!" I shoot back. "This is *his* car. *He* needed it for something, and we took it away. You think that's fair?"

Running on nothing but sugar from snacks—what was left after purging the contents of my belly—left me tired in a hurry, but I'm still far from calm. Part of me wants to bail out of the car, regardless of how fast we're going.

"Don't give me that," Sam scoffs. "I won't justify it or talk about what's 'fair'. That guy's needs versus our needs, it's pointless. Now we have the car. Isn't Alice what matters most?"

"He could have killed us, Sam," I say. "That matters. Is that the happy ending you want?"

"At any cost," Sam says, side-stepping the question. "I want to get us there no matter what and that's the end of it."

I can't believe what I'm hearing. If I had known what I was agreeing to when I let Sam come along this morning...

"This morning," I whisper, "you said you wanted to do something for yourself, in a way. Why did you really come with me?"

"I knew you'd face tough choices on the road," Sam replies. "I knew you wouldn't be able to make them. You're too fucking *nice*, Nate. Not a whole lotta love for thy neighbor today of all days. Plenty of people out here looking to take advantage of the situation. So, I wanted to be there, to do what you couldn't, shit like this. I tried to poison my dad. I killed my own dog. Whatever place good people go was already going to turn me away at the door, regardless of how today went down. What I do today, no matter how bad, is just the gravy on top of my shitty life. Figured it wasn't fair for you to share the same fate based on one bad day."

The low rumble of the road beneath our wheels rules the rest of the conversation. I don't know what else to say. In silence, a sign passes by, informing that we are back on track to Toronto, but that it's a ways off. With Sam at the helm, how much tribulation lay in wait between here and there? How many more promises to each other, to ourselves, would we have to break to get to Alice? Was it worth it?

Tip #10: Stay in touch. You never know what your last words might be

7 Hours Remaining

There are no more cars on the street. Everyone must have made it to where they needed to go. I picture a group of friends looking over past yearbooks and laughing, families huddled around a candle, praying in the dark, loved ones sharing one last intimate moment. The world is winding down to its end, and I'm out on the road, still trying to find a beginning.

D. J. Carlos, who has somehow stayed on the airwaves this entire time, sounds different. The man I hear coming through the speakers now isn't obnoxious or high-spirited at all. He sounds tired.

"I doubt anyone out there's still listening," he says, his radio persona completely shed. "That's probably a good thing. I hope you're all at home, or wherever you feel safe. That's why I'm here, still talking to you. D. J. Carlos, playing the hits you know and love…" There's a pause on the airwaves. "My name is Carlos Santos. I just turned thirty-six years old last week. My parents have been gone a long time, and I never started a family of my own. Figured I'd get around to it one day. That's the point of all this, right? To keep life going after you're gone? But to be honest with you, this gig is the only thing that ever made me happy. I never needed anything else. This studio, the people I worked with, they were my family. This was my home. My producer tells me we're going to lose broadcasting capabilities soon, so this is it. If even one person out there hears this, know that it was my pleasure playing the hits you know and love. Here's the final song, just for you."

I know the song from the first chord. *Good Riddance*. I always found the song to be old, cheesy and overplayed, but for some reason, in this moment, it nails every note, plucking at my heartstrings like the guitar in Billie Joe's hand. The lyrics, the melody, things I've heard a thousand times, hitting me like it's the first time.

> *For what it's worth, it was worth all the while.*
> *I hope you had the time of your life.*

When the song finishes, nothing but static plays over the radio.

"Just had to end it on a stupid song."

I turn to Sam and in the glow of the dashboard lights, I can see tears streaking down his cheeks.

"You know what's fucked up?" he asks. "No texts or calls from anyone, not one all day. Nothing from dad, big surprise. I thought maybe mom, wherever she is. Not Daniel, or Travis. I've got no one."

"You have me," I whisper.

For some reason, that just makes him bitter. He shrugs and wipes the tears on the sleeve of his shirt.

"Ah, who cares?" he mutters. "Phone full of 'friends,' ex-lovers, and not one reaches out, whatever. Another beauty about the end of the world: Wipes away all your exes."

At that moment, a text from Alice lights up my phone.

> Alice: *Nathaniel. Can I call you?*

Life hasn't been fair to Sam, for that there is no debate. I understand his frustrations, why the end of the world might be a nice change of pace for him, but for me, pain was worth the price of admission to this whole crazy show we found ourselves a part of. I refuse to let him think it was all a waste.

"Maybe I want my exes," I mutter.

"Huh?"

"That's what you don't get." I turn to my friend, letting the glow from my phone light up my face. "You like today for all the shitty things it wipes away, but maybe I wanted to go through the disappointment of not getting into the college I wanted, or finding out what it feels like to grow old. Maybe I wanted a taste of everything you're happy about losing. I wanted the opportunity to struggle, to fail, to lead a full life. Everything shitty sounds pretty good to me."

Sam stares at me like I have three heads, all speaking different languages at the same time. I don't know if what I said makes any sense, or if even a piece of it stuck with him, but I hope more than anything that by the end, Sam finds peace, even if I can't give it to him.

"Whatever," he replies. "I saw your phone go off. News from Alice?"

"She wants to call," I say.

"Go ahead."

We still have plenty of time between here and Alice's house. I'll be sure to revisit this conversation with Sam before we get there. In the meantime, I make the call to Alice, and she answers between the first and second ring. Actually kind of slow for her.

"Nathaniel, is that you?" she asks.

"Yeah, sorry for going off the grid so long," I say. I don't even know where to begin. "A lot's happened. I'll tell you all about it when I get there. We're on the road now, though. Making good time, I think."

"I'm just glad you're okay," she says. "I was getting worried there. Felt like forever since I heard your voice."

On Alice's side of the call, I hear the sound of a passing car.

"Are you driving?" I ask.

"About that," she mutters, sounding guilty. "I may or may not have stolen my parents' car."

Sam and I look at each other, flabbergasted.

"You what?"

"After our last call cut out, I figured your phone had died and that you'd get back to me," Alice explains. "When that didn't happen, I got nervous. Just looking at the clock was driving me crazy, but not like my mom and dad, or my sisters. So, I bailed."

"Without saying good-bye?" I ask.

"Today's been nothing but one long, drawn-out good-bye." Alice sighs deeply, the kind usually followed by tears. The line goes quiet for a moment, and when she starts up again, her voice is all scraggly. "It's all I've been doing since we found out. After the hundredth time of telling your parents how much you'll miss them, how much your sisters mean to you, you just get numb. Reminiscing runs its course, quick. Maybe I'm a terrible person, but I wanted something new. Figured it was your turn to get a proper farewell."

A kind, caring individual with a cool disposition might

share their sympathies with the loss of one's parents, but Alice is the girl of my dreams, and thus, it's the end part that really rattles my cage.

"Wait. *You're* coming to see *me*?"

"Well, duh! You were taking *way* too long. World would have ended waiting on you to make a move. Literally. Where are you right now?"

I check the GPS on Olivia's phone. With so many phones in my possession, I feel like some expert hacker-man.

"We're on Weston Road right now," I tell her. "You know it?"

"I do. Might be tricky, but I'll get there."

At first, I'm overcome with a surge of joy, but something that's been eating away at me all day stops me from letting that happiness take shape. When I look to the clock, and the night-sky, I think about Alice's parents, waiting for her to come back, and all that joy rushes out. What if it's already too late for us and we don't even know it?

"Alice," I whisper. "You're really sure about all this? What if this was a mistake?"

"What do you mean?" she asks.

"I don't know. Even if we make it, we'll only have a few hours to do…I don't even know what. What if, like, you were right to stay with your family? What if me coming out to see you just made things complicated?"

"Complicated sounds a lot better than just sitting around waiting to die."

"But those are your parents, your sisters. That's your family. I'm just...words on a screen."

All I hear from Alice's side of the call is the sound of cars passing by. Sam slaps my arm to let me know I'm blowing it. It's not like I *wanted* to believe that today was nothing but a silly pipe-dream, but the end of the world isn't the Make-a-Wish Foundation. We might not make it. How many lives had I trampled over today, for nothing?

"Nathaniel," she says coolly. Nobody says my name better than her. "There was a text I wrote out right before I left, when I thought maybe something bad had happened and you wouldn't make it. I wrote, *'I'm not sure where you are, or if you'll ever even read this, but if you do, know that I spent my last moments on Earth looking for you. See you on the other side, Scissorhands.'* You know why I didn't end up sending it?"

If I wasn't in love with her before, this sealed the deal for sure. It takes me a solid ten seconds to realize I'm shaking my head no, which she obviously can't see, instead of vocally answering her question.

"No, why not?" I ask.

"Because I knew that I'd find you. There's no doubt in my mind that we'll be together—that at the end of the world, I'm going to meet the guy of my dreams. Weston Road. Be there soon, present in hand."

She hangs up before I get a chance to respond, which only makes me want to be with her more. Well played, Alice. Well played. I'm left biting my lip, and Sam rolls his eyes when he sees the look on my face.

"Jeez," he mumbles, shaking his head. His spirits seem temporarily lifted. Something about Alice and me brings the best out of him. "Wish I'd found someone that dedicated. Remember Rachel? Broke up with me because I got her too many presents for 'weird' anniversaries. Said I tried too hard. Who *doesn't* celebrate their four month anniversary?"

"Anniversary kind of means yearly, not monthly," I say. "Besides, you told us *you* broke up with *her* because she was too clingy."

"Yeah, well, that version of the story made me look better. Can't have you thinking I'm the messed up one."

"You do that all on your own, actually." I can't stop thinking of Alice, and the lengths she's gone to. What an idiot. A romantic, wonderful idiot. "Sam, what do you think of this girl you're risking your life for me to meet. Be honest."

"Brutally?"

"Savagely."

Sam grins and fakes a sigh.

"Let's just say if I didn't think she deserved you, this gun would be going up her ass sideways."

I do something I thought lost since parting with Ezra and Olivia: I laugh.

"Sounds like a Sam stamp of approval to me," I say. "You two will get along famously."

"Maybe I can squeeze a threesome out of this apocalypse yet," he says with a big yawn. "You, me and Alice. Scratch one off the bucket list. I call middle!"

Sam keeps rubbing his eyes, and he's having a hard time staying in his lane. He deserves a break after all that grand theft auto.

"Do you need a nap?" I ask. "You seem tired."

"Something about constantly being on the verge of dying

is exhausting," he replies, "but I'll be okay."

"Come on. I'll take over for a bit. Get some rest."

"I've pulled more all-nighters playing *Halo* than any other person still living on this god-forsaken planet. This is but a meagre challenge for the likes of me."

"Pull over."

"Fine."

That was easier than anticipated. He must be really tired. Sam pulls the car over to the side of the road and puts it in park. I unbuckle my seatbelt, scooch over the center console and plop into the driver's seat as Sam stretches out for a nice nap. He leans the chair back and kicks his feet up onto the dashboard.

"I better have some kick-ass, outlandishly erotic last dreams or I'll feel supremely short-changed," he says. "Wake me up when we get there. Good-night and good-luck my good-lad."

Sam's out like a light before I have a chance to put the car in motion.

******

Half an hour of driving in the dark with nothing but Sam's snores for company puts weird thoughts in my head, the kind I sometimes get right before I fall asleep. Sitting in darkness like this, with only so many hours left in my life, comes a quiet panic, a panic I haven't experienced since dad's funeral.

I'm walking up to the casket, and I know he's in there, but I hope for things to be different. All the consequences of seeing him in there, like *that*, play out, and they're all bad, but I can't turn around now. Everyone's watching, expecting me to react in some specific way. Am I supposed to cry? Look away? But I just stand there, looking down at him.

Mom said it would look like he's sleeping, but it doesn't look like he's sleeping at all. No one's that still.

I haven't thought about that in a really long time.

I don't want to think about it anymore, but I don't want to wake Sam up either. Who would be awake at this hour to keep me company? I can only think of one person to share words with in the dark.

With the click of one button, I'm back in touch with Alice. I put the call on speaker phone so I can keep my hands free. I'm sure she's done the same.

"Couldn't wait to meet me in person, huh?" she says with a flirtatious drawl. "So impatient, Nathaniel."

"Trying to fit as many conversations as I can into my rapidly dwindling schedule, like speed-running a relationship" I tell her. "No, I've just been having weird thoughts. Needed someone to talk to."

"I know what you mean. Weird to think that around this time yesterday, you were drunk and we were talking about a first kiss."

The thought of that kiss makes my face hot.

"You still owe me one," I say. "But yeah. Everything changed so fast. Did I ever tell you how my dad died?"

"Heart-attack."

"That was like this. Every day feels the same for such a long time that you think, 'this is what life is like, always.' And then he died, and life turned into something else…Are you scared to die, Alice?"

Alice pauses for a moment. I get like this when I'm tired, all rambly. She's probably just trying to pick a target to aim her response at.

"I used to be," she says. She laughs a little. "This sounds

stupid, but I had this weird like, less than quarter life crisis when I was nine years old. I watched *Up* or some shit and realized what death was. Like, what it *really* was. My mom had to turn the movie off because I was crying so hard. For some reason I thought death was something that would only happen to me, and everyone would get to go on and make all these memories without me. I'd be stuck forever in nothingness while the world kept going. That haunted me for a long time. But now, I get it. Even if this black hole had never happened, we all go out one way or another. We all end up in the same place, even if that place is nowhere. It's nothing to be scared of. That kind of sounds bleak, when I say it out loud."

"No," I whisper. "No, it sounds good. Alice?"

"Yeah?"

"I'm terrified."

"I know. It's okay."

"If I were with you right now, I'd kiss you."

It's like we're back in my bed, whispering to each other, our heads on the same pillow. I picture her wide, beautiful smile, her hair, a little too long, tickling my face. We'll be that close, for real, soon enough.

"I can't wait," she says. "Good-bye, Nathaniel."

"Good-bye, Alice. See you soon."

The call ends with a loud beep that awakens Sam from his snoring slumber. I wipe the tears from my eyes before he notices. He coughs a few times and groggily sits up in his seat, ensuring his margarine container is still tucked tight under his arm. He wipes drool from the side of his mouth and pinches the bridge of his nose.

A long time passes before one of us breaches the silence.

"Had a dream that we never made it out of that mist, back

in the field," Sam whispers. "The black hole came…and it hurt."

"It was just a dream," I reply.

Tip #11: The world ends. Love doesn't. Never give up

5 Hours Remaining

I can't take my eyes off the clock. Midnight is long gone, and with it, the threshold has passed. A dim light on the horizon announces a new coming day. That day, today, March 22nd, is the day the world ends. In a few short hours, everything will cease to be. To someone else, far away in the cosmos, we'll just be one less thing to look at in the night sky.

This is taking too long.

"Remember that challenge I've been showing you?" Sam asks. He's using his phone to surf the web again. "#See You on the Other Side. I think we have a winner."

He tilts the phone in my direction and I cautiously let my eyes wander from the road. It's a GoPro video of someone in the back of a helicopter, looking down on the black hole from above. The adrenaline junkie gives the camera a thumbs-up before diving out into the air. Headfirst, this crazed person plunges fearlessly into the abyss, hooting and howling the whole way down. The darkness rises up fast, and just before the feed cuts out, there's a great hum, followed by a deafening whir. Just like when my mom was taken.

"I'm still gonna try to beat that though," Sam whispers with a sly grin. "No idea how, but I'll think of something."

"Where was that taken?" I ask.

"On the coast. It's close."

A deep shudder goes through me. Not long now until I hear that great hum first-hand. Thankfully, we're getting close.

I see the familiar red glow of tail-lights up ahead. Haven't seen those in a while. Silly of me to think that everyone was off the road already. I gently bring the car to a stop and start the waiting game. We've been lucky so far when it comes to traffic, but we were bound to run into some eventually. Hopefully this is just a temporary delay. The last one.

"Nate," Sam mutters.

I'm not really listening. I poke my head out the window to see what's causing the hold-up. A truck is stalled in the middle of the road, smoke pouring out from under its hood. Reminds me of my car back in the farmer's field.

"Nate," Sam says again, louder. His tone—thoughtful and brooding–catches my attention. "Listen. Before we meet Alice, I want to give you a choice."

A woman steps out into my headlights from behind the truck, waving at us. She seems friendly, older with white hair and a denim jacket. Most importantly, she's alone. I look to the other cars ahead of me. Why did no one get out to help her?

"Nate?"

"Yes, Sam, what is it?" I snap. I look over to him, his shaggy hair over his eye, giving me that beaten down stare, and pull back a little. "Sorry, what is it?"

"If you want me to go so you can enjoy your time alone with Alice, I'd understand," he says. "I'm not the best company. I don't want to ruin your perfect moment."

I don't know what brought that out, or why now, but the woman is nearly at my window and she looks like she wants to talk. Sam will have to wait.

"Forget it," I tell him quietly. "You're staying. The three of us will have a great time. Now can you please focus on this creepy lady outside my window?"

Dawn is coming, but it's still cold out. I can see the old woman shaking as she approaches my door. I immediately feel bad about calling her creepy. She wears a desperate smile, the kind you feel compelled to help.

"I'm so sorry to stop you like this," she says, her voice warm and tender. "I'm sure you're in a hurry. My name's Helena. I was out getting medicine for my husband when the truck gave out on me. It's his truck, really, and I never know how to deal with it on the best of days. I've tried everything but can't get it to start."

"Sorry, we're not very good with cars," I say. "Mine died yesterday and we just kind of left it."

"Isn't this your car?" she asks, pointing at the silver Corvette. Sam and I say nothing. She's suspicious, but not enough to delve further. "No matter. I don't mind leaving the truck behind. I live nearby, you see, and my husband's probably worried sick waiting for me. I know it's a lot to ask, but is it possible for you to drive me up the road a bit? It won't take long."

Sam is looking out his window at the cars idling between us and Helena's stalled truck with great suspicion.

"Again, sorry," I say. "This only seats two, and we really are in a hurry."

"Oh, come now," Helena says with a smile. "Are you really going to leave an old lady at the side of the road, today of all days? I don't have a phone. Can I at least borrow one of yours to call him?"

"Why don't you ask any of them?" Sam asks, pointing to the cars ahead of us. "They have room."

Helena looks back at the other cars and laughs a little. She looks back at me and says nothing. She just stares at me, like she's biding time. The hair on the back of my neck starts to rise and my heart hammers in my chest. Something's wrong.

I flip on the Corvette's high-beams and my breath is stolen away. The cars ahead are without passengers. Slinking up on each side of the road like hyenas in the night are men dressed in denim shirts, the same as Helena's. They're carrying hunting rifles and shotguns, all aimed right at our car. We're trapped.

A million actions—slamming my foot on the gas, running them over, switching the car into reverse, bolting on foot and never looking back—all feel like they'll end in a hail of bullets. I have to play this precisely right, or we're dead.

"Why are you doing this?" I ask, keeping my eyes forward at the men coming closer. "Do you have any idea what's going on out—"

"Please turn off your vehicle and step on out," Helena says.

I look up at her through the open window and see that her 'frail-old-lady' routine was all an act. She's as cold and uncaring as a winter's night.

"Just let us go," I plead.

"Come on now, get out," Helena commands. "Don't make a thing of it."

They've got the car surrounded. I want to look to Sam for guidance, but I'm too afraid to take my eyes off Helena and her gang. We're so close, and after everything we've been through, I can feel Alice slipping away.

"There's this girl—"

"That's nice," Helena interjects. "Keys please."

With that, I know my answer. Love has no power here. There's only one thing behind those hard eyes, and it has nothing to do with kindness. Maybe she knows this is the end, and this is how she's choosing to spend it. No matter what, I'm not getting out of this.

"What would God think about what you're doing?" I ask with tears in my eyes.

The men around the car laugh at me, but not Helena. She sighs and leans against the car, like I'm giving her the hard time.

"You a Catholic kid?" she asks. I nod proudly, scraping the tears away. "Figured. Always complicate things, the religious types."

I feel another presence to my side who isn't Sam. One of Helena's men is reaching over the passenger side door for the car keys, and there's nothing I can do to stop him. Sorry, Alice. Sorry you fell for someone so weak. Words on a screen, we remain.

"Let me tell you somethin', sweetie, that'll make life a whole lot simpler," she says. "God don't give a rat's ass about today any more than yesterday. You're out here, alone. Now get outta the damn car."

As the man's fingers wraps around the keys, Sam swiftly grabs the man by the collar, pulls out his gun, and sticks the barrel up into the man's ribs. No hesitation. My eyes gravitate straight to the trigger. This time, I don't stop him.

The ear-splitting shot is immediately followed by a burst of blood. My senses spike hard at first, but then the world fades to a dull ringing. I can see it all: bright stars, lonely road, the players and the gun. That moment hangs there in front of me, like a painting stuck in time for only me to admire and abhor.

Kind of beautiful, in a horrible way.

In that suspended space, with death so close, my own instinct emerges. It rages and rises to the surface, and everything becomes clear. This is what it takes. This is what it takes to get to Alice.

The man's blood runs down my face as he slumps backward and falls lifelessly away from the car. My foot's on the pedal before he hits the ground. Helena backs away from the car and yells at her gang to open fire. I try to steer around the car parked in front of me, but there isn't enough room. I clip the car's back bumper and get stuck. The smell of burning rubber fills the air as I attempt to brute force my way through.

Another shot lights up the night, this one aimed at us.

Bullets pierce the car on Sam's side, shattering his window. Glass and blood fly across the dashboard. Sam screams. He's been hit, I know it, but I can't turn to look. I flip the Corvette into reverse and swerve sideways, throwing the weight of the car into Helena. The front bumper slams into her hip and she's sent flying. Two down.

Unfortunately, I missed the guy with the shotgun. He takes aim at me right through the windshield and fires.

It takes me a moment to realize that I haven't been shot. I can't see through the smashed windshield, so I start driving blind. With a bit of extra wiggle room, I maneuver around the parked car in front of me and put the pedal to the floor. The car bounces over a body, maybe Helena's, and accelerates toward the man with the shotgun. He fires off another round just as I plow into him.

A gaping hole opens in the windshield from the buckshot impact, and I'm able to see again. Lucky for me, he misses. Unlucky for him, I don't.

The shotgunner tries to leap up and over the hood, but

his knees don't quite make the jump. He screams out in agony as he bounds off the bumper and is cast aside in a heap of broken bones.

The road ahead is clear, but I keep my head low because the remaining members of Helena's gang won't let us escape so easily. In the rearview mirror, I see a line of shadows trying to shoot us down. Bullets rip the back of the car apart, shattering my tail lights and windows.

Then comes a loud popping noise, like a bursting balloon, and suddenly it feels like I'm driving on bumpy ice. Slowing down isn't an option with our pursuers so close, but I can't keep the car straight. The Corvette starts to swerve uncontrollably. Panicking, I lay my hands off the wheel and let physics take over.

Physics decides that Weston is no longer hospitable and takes a sharp right. We fly off the road, over a ditch, and slam into a small grouping of trees. The car is probably too old for airbags, so instead, the steering wheel hits me like a swift punch to the face. Blood leaks from my possibly broken nose as I unbuckle my seatbelt and force my way out of the car.

Some kind of gas leaking from the car doesn't sit well in my lungs, causing me to gasp for air. I fall to the ground and hastily catch my breath before assessing the damage. The Corvette is totaled. Sam isn't out yet. If we stay here, they'll come for us. We have to keep moving.

I stumble through the underbrush and pry Sam's door open. He's covered in blood and wheezing, but still alive and holding on to that damn margarine container. I unbuckle his belt and sling his arm around my shoulders. My muscles scream for me to stop, to just drop him, but I fight through the pain and drag Sam from the wreckage.

"Not one person we met today was chill," Sam rasps.

"Stop talking."

The woods around Weston aren't particularly thick, but they extend back pretty far. Plus, we still have the cover of darkness on our side for a little while longer. Our best option is to delve into the woods and hope that Helena's gang doesn't find us. Scariest game of hide and seek I've ever played.

With Sam practically slung over my shoulders, we abandon the car with all our stuff inside and trek into the wilderness. I do this knowing full well that Sam will probably bleed out soon. I do this with the knowledge that Alice will never find me.

Sun's coming up soon.

Tip #12: Whether a bang or a whimper, go out the way you want to

3 Hours Remaining

So, this is it. Patches of grass at our feet, trying to recover from a long winter. Surrounded by wild trees with twisted branches that have probably only ever been seen by a handful of humans. Leaning up against a fallen tree covered in a comfy moss. A bird's nest above, abandoned. Quiet. Not a bad place to die.

We've given up hiding, though I can't even be sure Helena's gang ever chased after us. It doesn't matter. With Sam's wound, we're not going anywhere. His stomach and chest look like they've run through a cheese grater. He moans in pain, which makes him cough up blood, which causes more pain. There's nothing I can do for him. At least he's still got his margarine container.

"An old lady," Sam scoffs. More coughing. More blood. Not that any of it will actually shut him up. "And her Neanderthal friends. Never thought I'd get killed by an old fucking lady."

"Don't say that," I groan. My face and arms are throbbing. "You'll be fine."

"Um, I'm no doctor, but I'm pretty sure this is what they'd call 'fatal.' If there is an afterlife, the Wi-Fi better be fast and free. A man needs his memes, dead or alive."

My pocket vibrates and I jump a little. Miraculously, my phone has somehow survived a shootout and a crash. They should've put that in the marketing. I gingerly retrieve it despite my aching body scolding me to stop moving so much. My Alice-senses are tingling.

➢ Alice: *On Weston. Where are you?*

I can't bear to reply. I've wasted the last months of her life. She could've been falling in love with someone real, someone right in front of her that she could touch and hold. Instead, she's on a wild goose chase for a guy who's about to die in the woods along with his best friend, holding a margarine container full of god knows what. It's all so ridiculous.

"We tried," I croak, putting my phone away. "We tried. We just didn't have enough time."

Sam lets the margarine container slip from his hands so that he can grab my arm.

"Not good enough," he wheezes. "You have to see her. You *have* to. Or else I die for nothing."

"Don't put that on me. You can't."

"Oh, I'm putting that on you. You see Alice, or my entire existence is meaningless. There. That should light a nice toasty fire under your ass."

I look to the holes in Sam's chest and sigh. There's no point in arguing. For his peace of mind, I'll just smile and nod. He won't live long enough to know it's a lie.

"Okay," I whisper. "I'll try."

"Good."

Sam sits up a little and tenderly withdraws something small from his back pocket. An old iPod, with tangled up earbuds.

"Where'd you pull that from?" I ask.

"My butt," he replies.

Sam's voice cracks and he starts coughing so hard I'm afraid he won't stop. This crazy asshole literally took a bullet for me, and I've been brushing him off all day like a needy pet. I don't deserve a friend like Sam.

"Remember how we met?" I ask.

"Oh, Jesus Christ," he groans. "Are you about to get sappy on me? It feels like you are."

"Shut up. Grade nine, Mr. West's class, and his seating plan had me stuck right next to you. People said you smelled like the worst weed, that you spent every lunch listening to metal music by yourself."

"What a lovely legacy to leave. You must have been super hyped to have me as a desk-mate."

"To be honest, I was a little nervous. But on the first day of class, I sat next to you, ready for a year of smelly weed and heavy metal. And I don't know how or why it happened, but I tooted badly. Like, it was fierce."

"It was pretty fucking nasty."

"But you didn't say anything. You didn't laugh or make fun of me like anyone else would. You just looked over at me and shrugged. I knew right then that everyone had you wrong."

"Who knew a fart could bring people together?"

Sam and I laugh, despite the immense pain it causes him. If I leave, he'll die alone, but if I stay, Alice will spend her last moments wondering where the hell I went. I want to punch myself. How can I possibly think about Alice with my best friend dying in front of me?

"I'm sorry for freaking out at you over stealing the car," I mutter, angry tears in my eyes. "I don't know what I was thinking. You were just trying to help. I've been nothing but ungrateful and shitty to you this whole time—"

"It's what I was here to do, remember?" he says with a smile. He pops an earbud in and looks for a song to die to. "So don't worry about it, Nate. I mean, keep crying, because that makes me feel nice. Never had someone cry for me, ya know? Makes me feel special and shit."

"I was so caught up in Alice this whole time, I feel like… like I just used you."

"Hey, I picked this. I could've left your ass back at school, gone home to smoke a bowl, maybe hooked up with some hot stranger, and waited for all this to end, but I thought, 'you know what would be more fun? Getting shot.' This was the right choice, and I'm glad I made it."

Sam finds his song and presses play. I can't see the name, but it has an immediate effect on him. He picks at his collar and lets his hair slide into his eyes—blackened from the car crash. He's trying to keep things light, but I can see him slipping back into who he used to be before he knew the world was over.

"When I woke up and found out what was happening, I got so damn excited," he whispers, looking to the sky. "Everything I ever wanted, without having to pull the trigger. I was free. Now that it's here…it really sucks. I was wrong. I want all those things you said; growing old and all that 'full life' crap. Everything shitty sounds swell to me too. I should've done more when I had the chance. I guess… I just thought I wasn't good enough to get them, ya know?"

This time, I don't have to lie.

"You are."

I take his hand and squeeze as hard as I can. A faint smile crosses his lips, but his breath becomes shallow. Lightly, he squeezes back.

"You dork. Don't get soft on me. Remember, I did this for myself. Not for you."

Sam winks at me. I throw my head back to laugh and the sun gets in my eyes…

Wait a minute. Can it be? Through the cracks between the trees come soft rays of light. I close my eyes and let it wash over me. It feels like an eternity has passed since I last felt the warm kiss of day.

As beautiful a gift as this dawn is, I know that the end of everything comes with it.

"Sun's up," I whisper. "Welcome to the last day on planet earth, Sam. Sam?"

No crass remark. No internet reference. Silence tells me he's gone, but I squeeze his hand anyway. I nudge his shoulder and call out his name, but he's gone. No way is another friend leaving me without a proper good-bye.

"Bet this makes you feel all special and shit," I gasp. "Probably died on purpose just to get a reaction."

If Helena's gang did stumble upon me, they likely would leave me alone. Talking to a dead guy? They'd think me insane. And maybe I am. A little insanity at the end of the world can't hurt.

I go to put the margarine container back in his lifeless hands and stop. The lid is open. There's some kind of grey dust inside.

"Ashes?"

The story of Chester comes back to me, along with all the memories of Sam holding that small dog close to his chest, just like the margarine container. Sam must have lied when he said he buried him. Oh...

I start to cry, quietly at first, but the sadness that envelops my body is so intense it scares me. My soul starts to crack. I don't know how else to explain it. Like, no matter what good there is left in the world, I'll never be able to experience it the same now that I've felt this way. I feel fractured.

Fighting back tears, I start scratching at the cold ground, figuring that Sam needs to be buried. It's what he deserves. My nails start to bleed. He never got that when he was alive. The ground's still frozen from the winter. I owe him this much.

My phone vibrates again, and I stop. I don't need to check, but I have to make a decision. If I don't leave Sam right now, I definitely won't make it to Alice in time. It really will have all been for nothing.

I pound my fist into the dirt and unleash a torrent of colourful curses. It's about the only thing I can do. It's shitty and not fair at all, but if anyone could appreciate that, it's Sam.

I stand up in a huff and take a step away from that shallow grave. In the dead quiet of the woods, I can hear music playing in Sam's ear. I don't know the song, but it sounds beautiful. The sweet, soft melody calms me down a bit. Hopefully, wherever he is, Sam can hear it too.

He can keep the music, but the gun is coming with me. Something tells me I might need it. I kneel down to take it from him, and cross his arms over that margarine container so tight he'll never let it go. When the black hole comes for him and Chester, they'll go out together.

I stuff the gun into my waistband and get ready to leave, but something keeps me there. I need to say something, even if no one's there to hear it.

"So," I whisper with a lump in my throat. "This...This is how the story of Sam ends. Best damned friend I ever had."

That's as far as I get. It's not enough, but I can't say anymore. Words are just words. How he lived, how many times he made me laugh and saved my ass today alone...I can't tell that story. It was a privilege to be a part of it.

I think back to all my friends and family. My mom. Travis, Dan. Olivia and Ezra. Sam. Everything they did, helped me get this far. Sam was always worried about what he did or didn't deserve, but in that moment, I was confident in knowing that I *definitely* didn't deserve such kind people in my life. I might just be the luckiest person left on the planet.

Before I know it, I'm walking away from his body. With every step, I know he's disappearing behind me, that I'll never see him again. Don't turn back, Nate. It'll just make it worse. Don't turn back.

******

Without Sam around, I have to rely on myself for protection. The woods are quiet, but every time a branch snaps or a bird tweets, I nearly shoot something. My phone hasn't vibrated in a bit, but I'm not checking any messages until I'm in the clear. Only problem is that I'm not going back to Weston Road. Helena's gang could still be on patrol.

I remember seeing another road on the GPS next to Weston called Pine Valley. Once I find my way there, I'll text Alice ...ah, shit. She might run into Helena's gang first if I don't tell her to course correct. I can't put it off any longer.

I find the tree with the thickest trunk and use it for cover and pray no one catches me with my metaphorical pants down. I can hear Olivia droning in my ear, telling me how this is not the time for texting. This damn well *is* the time for texting. Oh, great. I'm arguing with myself. The blood loss from my wounds must be worse than I think.

My inbox is flooded with messages from Alice and my service provider offering some excellent end of the world deals. I scroll up to the most recent message.

➢   Alice: *Looks like some kind of roadblock up ahead. Looks shady as hell. You see this?*

I'm caught in a panic so severe that my fingers won't co-operate. It's like I'm drunk again. I can't spell for shit and auto-correct doesn't pick up the slack.

➢   Me: *Do NOT approach. Get off Weston immabmitelely. Headto Pine Valley. I'll meet you there*

Close enough to proper English. I hit 'send' and the little loading circle starts spinning. And spinning. And spinning.

Suddenly, my cell loses all reception. 'Message sending failed, please try again.' No, please. I wait for the signal to come back, but it doesn't. It can't be. Not yet.

I jump to my feet and start wandering around in circles, hoping that I'm just in a bad area, but my cell still reads no bars. I quickly turn it off and on to see if it was a problem with the SIM card, but the signal's gone for good.

I look around and begin to understand. Either the satellite or the tower for my area has just been consumed by the creeping darkness. My heart falters and my mouth goes dry. The end is near. I'm out of time.

My mind spins off in a million different directions. What if Alice didn't get the message and gets caught while I putter around Pine Valley? What if she *did* get the message and I go back to Weston for nothing? What if I go back and get caught by Helena's gang too? Then, at least, we'll die together. Morbid, but romantic.

Today, every minute counts as a year, and my time's up. That's all I can afford for the most important decision I'll ever make. Did Alice get the message or not? To my right—the way I came—is a deep darkness without end. Weston waits, and all the danger that comes with it. To my left, the trees thin out into a clearing. Pine Valley can't be far. Make a choice. Now or never.

The text went through. Alice got the message. I have to believe that's the case.

Just like with Sam, I don't look back. There's no time for second-guesses. Still, I need something to get my thoughts off the possibility that I just doomed Alice to a gang of monsters. The throbbing pain in my shoulder does the trick.

Every time my body screams at me to stop, Alice's smile flashes in my mind, pushing me that one extra step. The woods make way for a lonely road caught in a valley of pine. Fitting name.

I stumble out into the open like a zombie and scan each way. I spot one car, flipped over and set on fire. How does that always happen in apocalyptic settings? Other than that, the road's completely abandoned. She's not here. Great. I'm going to die one street over from the girl of my dreams. She didn't get the message. I chose wrong.

A terrible, unwanted memory emerges from the darkest part of my thoughts. Daniel, walking up the stairs, jumping off the school roof. The man in the car with a halo of blood over his head. Maybe they had the right idea. No moral quandaries inside a Corvette or creepy old ladies hijacking your car; never getting shot or watching their best friends die. Jumping certainly would have sped things up a bit.

Even if I leave for Weston now, I won't make it, and there's no guarantee that I'll even come out of the woods in the right place. It's done. All I can do now is wait—wait for the great whirring to take me away.

A gust of wind shakes the trees, awakening from their long winter slumber, and I'm blessed with the sound of shaking leaves, born just in time to witness the end of everything. These small gifts, soon to be gone forever. Did I appreciate them enough in the moment, before I knew it was for the last time? Why ever worry for the future when I have so much now to lose?

The wind dies down, and for a moment I'm alone again, but another sound soon takes to the airwaves. It's not like the great whir of the black hole, so I breathe easy for a moment, but this low hum steadily gets louder, and that's when I see it. A black blur barreling down the road, straight at me. Am I hallucinating?

The black blur takes shape in the form of an SUV. The same kind of car Helena's gang used to block Weston Road. Not hallucinating. They've come back for me. This time, I have nowhere left to run.

I stand my ground and raise Sam's gun in front of me. The driver must not be scared, because they don't swerve or slow down. Maybe they don't think I'll shoot. I prove them wrong.

The loud pop and sudden kickback of the first shot catches me off-guard. A complete miss, and the SUV is still playing chicken. I'll just pretend that was my warning shot. I bring my other hand forward for extra stability and fire two more rounds. They pierce through the hood and windshield of the SUV and force the driver to back down moments before smearing me across the pavement.

The SUV veers to the right and goes off the road, but pumps the brakes before slamming into a tree like I had. Those quick reflexes tell me that I missed my mark. The driver's still alive.

Cautiously, I circle around the back of the vehicle with my gun still drawn. I hear someone shuffling through shattered glass, and wait for the car door to open. The second they step out —no talking, no negotiating. Just a bullet, for Sam.

The car door pops open and I take a step back. There's

no telling if this person is armed. The driver sticks one arm out in surrender, but I'm not buying it. I circle around a bit more to catch a reflection in the rear-view mirror, but the angle's wrong. Is a human heart built to beat this hard? Maybe I'll just a have a heart-attack and get it over with.

"Come out!" I shout. "Keep your hands up!"

The sweat trickling down my forehead is getting blood in my eyes. I wipe it all away the best I can, keeping one eye open the whole time. The driver is slow to follow my command, and I hear more shuffling. Are they grabbing something? Please, let me be the faster gunslinger.

Finally, the driver puts one foot on the ground. Immediately, I notice something's off. Helena's gang was full of big, burly dudes in their forties. That's a *teenager's* leg.

Her other arm pokes out of the SUV and in her hand is a small, wrapped present. She steps out of the car wearing a nervous smile. My hands fall to my sides and Sam's gun rattles off the pavement. No fucking way.

"Is that how you greet all the girls you like?" Alice asks.

End of the world. Best friend just died. Bleeding out from a gunshot wound. Just shot at the girl of my dreams. *This* is a perfect moment.

Tip #13 : Don't wait. Don't make excuses. If you've found love, make it real, and don't let go

1 Hour Remaining

I can't believe it. After everything today's thrown at me, she's standing right there. She's real. Alice; on an empty road, with flames at her back and the wind in her hair. I'll take that image with me when I go.

"You just gonna stare at me over there or can we talk like human beings?" she teases, slowly putting her arms down.

"Shit, sorry, it's just—"

"I'm more gorgeous in person than you ever imagined? Sorry to steal your line."

"Kind of did, yeah."

There's that wide, beautiful smile I've written so many bad songs about. I didn't even notice that we've been walking toward one another the whole time we've been talking. She's close enough to touch. After five months trapped on the other side of a phone—and one hell of a bad day—I thought I'd never get this close. She's more stunning than pictures give her credit for.

"I thought my text didn't go through," I whisper.

"It did," she replies.

She looks to my bloody nose and gives me a look that says 'what the hell happened?'

"Eh, it's just a flesh wound," I say with a shrug. Shrugging hurts. "Got shot at. No big deal. Not the end of the world or anything."

"I see. Nice black eyes, by the way. Makes you look super badass."

"Kinda got into a car crash, too. I've been busy."

"Where's Sam?"

That was long enough for the fun part of the conversation, I suppose. I know that right now everything is bottled up, and the minute I pop the cork off, my emotions will explode. I hope she's ready for that. Alice must be able to tell something's wrong, because she frowns and bows her head a little.

"Sounds like you need to take a load off."

She walks back to her car and pops the hatch. Maybe she's got a spare shoulder brace kicking around. She pulls out a large case, and the jangling of glass tells me it's full of beer. Even better.

"Figured dying isn't as scary when you're buzzed," she says.

She puts the case down and rips off the lid. One for her, one for me.

"I like your style," I say.

I twist off the cap and take a nice, long sip. Tastes like it did last night, back when Olivia and Ezra were dancing under stolen fireworks—back when all of this was just another one of Jeremy's conspiracy theories.

"So," she says. "Tell me everything."

We gravitate to the upturned, flaming car as I fill in the blanks of what happened. Drinks by the fire just make sense. And there, by the fire, I tell her how Olivia and Ezra left to give me a chance. I show her the note they left for me. I tell her of the stolen car, and the road-block. I tell her the story of Sam, from the beginning. It hurts to tell, but the ending isn't so bad.

"He wanted to meet you so badly," I grumble. Please, don't cry in front of her. That's too much embarrassment for one day. "But he never got what he wanted, what he deserved, ya know? He had so much to give, but no one stopped to notice. His parents didn't give a shit, and his friends…I was his best friend and I was no better than anyone else."

"I don't think that's true," Alice replies. "You were there with him at the end, right? No one else can say that. Because of you, he wasn't alone."

Some guilt-prone part of my nature tells me to be combative, but the more I mull it over in my mind, the more I come to realize she's probably right. In my head, I did so many things wrong, but then Alice looks at me, and I know I wouldn't trade a second of that horrible journey away. Maybe having someone by your side at the end really is the best we can hope for. She has a way with words, this girl of my dreams.

"My mom would've liked you," I say.

"You think so?"

"Definitely. She was a sap, like you. Like me."

Alice's laugh sounds so satisfied, content, like she's grateful just to be happy. It's a heart-warming sound, or maybe I'm just starting to get drunk.

"Wish I could've met her," she says.

Talking about my mom sparks a memory I nearly forgot. Much to Alice's confusion, I tug my shoe off and pull out the picture I swiped from my house yesterday morning. It's a little crumpled from the journey, but the essence of that proud mother next to her son on his birthday remains intact.

"Here," I say. "That's her."

"She's beautiful."

"Isn't she?"

"So that's where you got your looks from."

"I'm sure my dad had something to do with it, too." We stare at each other for a little while, just enjoying the silence. It's not awkward with her, like I worried it might be. After months of long pauses between texts, actually being able to see her makes the time go by even faster. "What about you? What did you get from your parents?"

She hums for a moment, thinking on an answer I can tell she already knows. There's a slight shade of red on her cheeks. Embarrassed, perhaps?

"My romantics, for sure," she finally replies. "The only people my parents have ever been with is each other, since like high-school. I don't know. The fact that they spent all those years together and still find ways to surprise and laugh with each other, that stuff stuck with me. Maybe set up unrealistic expectations about what a relationship is. Or maybe not. Maybe I got lucky when I found you."

She's so sweet that I can feel my teeth rotting out of my head. I love it, every second of talking to her. For a moment, I forget that the world is about to end, that soon, it will be like this conversation never happened. No one will be alive to remember any of this, and I couldn't care less. This is the happiest I've ever been.

"Maybe I should call them one last time before the black hole comes," she says with tears in her eyes. "I talked to them basically the whole way here. They were mad at first, me sneaking out like that, but in the end I think they understood. What they had with each other, they wanted for me. What do you think? Should I call or...?"

She doesn't know it's already too late. At the end of the world, you get pretty good at being the bearer of bad news.

"It's close," I tell her. "Very close. The tower is already down in this area. You won't get reception...I'm sorry, Alice."

Panic grips Alice. She looks at me like I might be kidding, or that she might be able to barter her way out of this situation. I let her place her head on my shoulder and squeeze her arm. That's what I must have looked like when my mom was ripped away from me.

"Gotta admit," she mutters, wiping her eyes. "Didn't picture our first date quite like this. Thought maybe dinner and a movie. Something simple. Didn't expect so much crying... any crying actually."

"Could've been a sad movie," I reply.

"Well, this is much better than a sad movie."

Her smile is better than the wind, more beautiful than the sunrise. A tiny screen doesn't do it justice.

I barely even notice the black hole creeping over the horizon.

It doesn't sink in, not right away. After all, the black hole is something that happened to people far away. Like a black wave it washes over the world at an unwavering pace. It eats the very road I stand on, the trees in the distance, the clouds in the sky, and everything else my eyes can see. At this rate, it'll be here in less than five minutes.

"You'll be the last thing I see before the world goes dark," I whisper. "Can't think of a better way to say good-bye to this life."

Alice reads my eyes, but doesn't turn around.

"It's here, isn't it?" she whispers, knowing the answer. I nod. "There's no time. I wish we had more. You didn't even get to open your present!"

We fall into each other's arms and what seemed so impossible just hours ago, finally happens. We touch, fully embraced. Everything snaps into place. With her head against my chest, I'm not scared, or lost to the approaching storm. I get it. I'm okay.

"I don't," I say. "I don't care about presents, or anything else I supposedly missed out on. All day, everyone's been wishing for more time, regretting the things they'll never do, but now I get it. I don't wish we had a thousand lifetimes or even a second more. All I wanted was this moment, together, and I have it. We have now, we have each other, and that's enough. Now is everything."

There's no future where we get married and have a family and retire by the coast. There's only this: This day, this road, this girl of my dreams, leaning in for this perfect kiss. And when our lips touch, it feels like a goddamn fireworks display; colours bursting behind my eyelids, sparks scattering across my lips, every inch of my body rocketing into the sky. I can't help but smile. Everything was worth it for that one moment. Top that, black hole.

"Nathaniel, that was one hell of a first kiss," Alice says

after catching her breath.

She's absolutely right, so I lean in for another.

There are a million little details to take in, like the smell of her hair, or the softness of her lips. All these tiny wonders I could never bring to life from pictures, pieced together in front of me to create someone so real and vibrant. If I could freeze a single moment forever, it would be this one.

But then comes the hum.

There it is. That relentless whirring sound I've heard all day, but now it's here, coming for me. We have less than a minute. The black tide is right behind Alice, erasing everything that ever was.

"I'm not ready!" she cries out.

"Just don't look back!" I tell her. "And don't let go!"

The world around us slips away until there's nothing left but this stunning girl who once liked an Instagram photo. A supercut of my life plays out—from that blindingly white kitchen to now, holding her hand. I've never felt so alive.

"I'm so glad I was wrong!" I shout over the whirring.

"About what?" she shouts back.

"You are so much more than just words on a screen!"

The darkness consumes us just like every other soul on the planet, and in the blink of an eye, everything is gone. Silence.

See you on the other side.

ACKNOWLEDGEMENTS

I would like to take this page to thank everyone that was instrumental in the creation and release of How to Meet a Girl. To Mandy, thank you for capturing the mood and setting the stage for the story with your wonderful cover. To my sister, Shannon, who read one of the earliest incarnations of this story and helped shape it into what it is now. To my father, Mark, who listened to me prattle on about this book, and many others, for countless hours. To my mother, Deborah, who has read these pages more than I have and believed in its magic even when I did not. To my wife, Marlee, who gave me most of my best ideas (yes, the butter was all her). To all my friends and family who put up with my ridiculous dreams. To all the people on Twitch who watch my silly antics, you all rock. To everyone who read this book. I hope to see you all for the next one.

ABOUT THE AUTHOR

Christopher Compton

Christopher Compton has been writing stories for as long as he can remember and shows no sign of stopping. He streams daily on Twitch.tv under the name Endless Backlog. He lives in Ontario, Canada with his wife, Marlee, and their dog, Daisy.

Printed in Great Britain
by Amazon